TRAMP'S BRIDE

MAIL ORDER BRIDES OF TEXAS BOOK FOUR

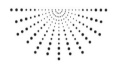

KATHLEEN BALL

This book is dedicated to Heather Crispin, Leeanne Turley and everyone else at the Livin' Large Farm. It's really become my home away from home. A big thank you to all the authors in The Pioneer Hearts Group on facebook. And to Bruce, Steven, Colt and Clara because I love them.

CHAPTER ONE

rging Jack, his bay quarter horse, forward until they reached the spot he'd yearned for, Tramp Hart then pulled on the reins slowing his mount, to a stop. From his location on top of a hill, he could see the expanse of the ranch, a ranch he'd helped to build. He'd been gone over a year, and he wasn't sure what type of reception would be waiting for him.

The ranch looked great. Better than great. There were plenty of cattle and a few more houses on the property. Cinders always seemed to have a magical touch with both horses and cattle. Tramp felt bad the way their friendship had ended. He sure hoped he'd be able to mend fences. He needed to be home.

Taking a fortifying breath, he loosened the reins and pointed Jack in the direction of the main house. One of the new houses on the property was the design he and Cinders had planned for his home. He did own a quarter of the ranch and had been foreman until he'd left. A smile spread over his face. Cinders must have known he'd be back. But despite the smile, the lump in his throat remained.

1

He dismounted, tied Jack to the wood railing, and slowly walked up the steps to Cinders' house. He hesitated before knocking taking a moment to close his eyes and hope he'd find himself welcomed. He knocked and waited but no one answered. In the old days he'd have just walked in but not now.

With hat in hand he walked across the yard to his house. He opened the front door and it surprised him to see it furnished. Cinders had always been a generous friend. He'd take a quick look around and then brush down Jack. Taking his hat off, he nodded, admiring the workmanship on the house. He walked farther inside and stopped short. There in the kitchen stood a willowy, dark-haired woman. She wore her hair up but a good amount of it had escaped, and a few enchanting ringlets hung down. She was busy making candles. He couldn't help but notice how lovely she was.

She jerked her head up and her mouth formed an O. "Listen mister, I don't want any trouble with you. I have a shotgun and I ain't afraid to use it."

Tramp peered around and didn't see a gun let alone a shotgun. "What are you doing in my house?" he asked annoyed at the way she stared at him.

"Your house? I think you have the wrong idea cowboy. The bunkhouse is just to the left of *my* house. So, if you don't mind, I have to finish dipping these here candles and hang them to dry. Good day." She went back to her candles making him feel as welcome as a polecat at a picnic.

He ran his fingers through his hair and frowned. "I do believe there's some type of mistake made. This is my house—"

"Nope, absolutely not. Now please leave." She hung the candles she was working on to dry and the next thing he knew, he was looking down the barrel of a shotgun. "Git!"

He instantly put his hands up. "Listen Miss— Heck, I

didn't get your name. I'll just leave you be until Cinders comes back."

"It's Ilene, Ilene Duffy"

"I'm Tramp." He saw a spark of recognition in her eyes. "See ya around." Offering a polite nod, he turned and walked back to the door, grabbing his hat on the way out. Perhaps Cinders hadn't wanted him to come back after all. He'd half expected it, but still his heart dropped.

The last year had been spent soul searching and mourning his friendship with Cinders. They'd grown up together and they'd always had each other's back until Charlotte. She was the prettiest gal this side of the Mississippi and he had loved her with everything within him. He tried to be happy for Cinders and Charlotte when they wed. Heck, he was even the best man. *Some best man.*

Once his betrayal became known, he couldn't face Cinders anymore and he'd lit out. It ripped out his heart and his soul. He never realized how much his friendship with Cinders meant to him. Charlotte's grave was over yonder under a big cottonwood. He never could bring himself to visit it.

He'd known he was taking a chance coming back but he wasn't ready for the disappointment that coursed through him. He ambled over to Jack and untied the reins. "Looks like we're going to have to go on for a few more hours." He patted Jack's neck.

CINDERS SHOOK HIS HEAD. He must be seeing things. If he didn't know better he'd have thought the man at his house was Tramp. He watched from on top of his horse, observing as the man swept off his hat and ran his fingers through his dark hair. Cinders' heart beat painfully against his ribcage. It was Tramp. He'd know that cowpoke anywhere. He had a different horse but the way the man moved was all Tramp.

Spurring his horse, he kicked up dust as he galloped to the house. They came to a stop and he vaulted off the horse. "You old son of a gun!" Cinders ignored the hand Tramp held out and hugged him close instead. He'd worried about his friend every day and was relieved to have him home.

"I'm glad you're back." There was so much he wanted to ask but for now he'd let it be. The troubled expression on Tramp's face concerned him. "Well, come on in. Shannon will be thrilled to see you when she gets home. She's over at Keegan's place organizing some quilting thing. A bee I think they call it."

"Keegan got his own place?"

"Yes, and he's done well so far. Even snatched himself a wife. He has two children now."

"Twins?"

Cinders laughed. "No his filly already had a little filly of her own. They had a son they named Ryan about six months ago."

"What else have I missed?"

"Come on in and have some coffee. I'll catch you up." Cinders went up the porch steps and into the house with Tramp right behind him. "Careful not to trip over the baby things."

"Baby?"

Cinders went right to the cook stove and grabbed the coffee pot. He poured two cups and gestured for Tramp to have a seat. "Yes a baby," he said as he set the coffee in front of his friend. "Her name is Olivia. She's a week older than Ryan."

Tramp cleared his throat. "I missed an awful lot."

"You are planning to stay aren't you?" Cinders took a swig of coffee.

4

"Yes, no. I'd love the answer to be yes but I don't want to intrude. You seem happy enough without me. The ranch is thriving," Tramp said with a strange hitch in his voice.

"This isn't about being happy without you. You're family, and you've been missed. I put away a quarter of the earnings for you. I figured you'd need it sooner or later. I'd really like it if you could stay. The job of foremen is taken, but the job of partner isn't."

Tramp looked away and seemed to stare at the wall for a while. He took a deep breath and turned back to Cinders. "I'm still ashamed about my part in Charlotte's and your unhappiness. I still can't fully understand why I did it. I drove her to her lover's house and drove her home. I covered for her. It ate away at me but when you found out, it became a burden I couldn't carry."

"She had a lot of people fooled. She's gone now. I'm committed to Shannon, and she tells me she loves me every day." A smile slid across his face. He couldn't help it. He had everything he ever wanted. A loving wife, a beautiful daughter, and a prosperous ranch. "Let's just put it behind us."

Tramp's shoulders relaxed and he momentarily closed his eyes. "Thank you. I had hoped to stay. I see you used the plans to build a house for that Ilene gal."

Chuckling Cinders nodded. "I built it so you'd have a home here. Ilene came out as a mail order bride. She grew up in the same building in New York City Shannon did."

"Oh, who's the lucky guy?"

Cinder's body tensed and he drew a steadying breath. "She was another of John Hardy's victims. He lured her here too and expected her to become a saloon girl instead of a wife. Oh, he ended up in jail, and someone killed him."

"Good riddance. Is the saloon closed now?"

Cinders laughed at the pained expression on Tramp's face. "It's still open. Noreen is the owner now."

Tramp's face relaxed and he almost smiled. "I always did like Noreen best. What else has been happening?"

"We have a new sheriff, Shane O'Connor and he recently got married. I know I've probably forgotten a heap of details but you'll be around. Dang, it's good to see your ugly mug!"

"It's surely nice to be welcomed. When will Ilene move out so I can move into my house?"

Cinders frowned and shook his head. "I really thought she'd have been married to another fella by now. We can wait for Shannon to come home."

"Why didn't Ilene go to the quilting tea?"

"Bee." Cinders frowned. "I think it's called a bee, but tea does make more sense."

ILENE COULDN'T HELP but peer out her front window at the handsome stranger. While she always thought Cinders to be the most handsome, with his blond hair and blue eyes Tramp was more pleasing to her eye. His dark, wavy hair hung down past his collar, and his brown eyes were ringed with amber. She thought him to be taller and wider than Cinders. Shaking her head she berated herself. He was a threat to her; he wanted her house.

Not that she had any claim to the house but she'd been living in it almost a year. Somehow she'd come to think of it as hers. Turning away from the window, she looked around the front room. Little by little she had exchanged pies and other baked goods for furniture and a bit of coin. None of the furniture had been new but she cleaned them up. Her favorite was a settee where she liked to sit and watch the sun go down. It'd been terribly torn up, but she'd covered it with canvas that she had dyed red, using the plant Indian paintbrush to create the dye. The red color had turned out well, and the results gave her a fine sense of accomplishment.

A chill went up her spine at the thought of losing it all. She'd had a few proposals, and now it looked as though she should have said yes to one of them. She never wanted to marry, but right now she'd have to put aside her wants and deal with the harsh reality. There was no doubt Tramp wanted his house.

Fear clutched her heart. Why hadn't she made more friends out here in Texas? Shannon had invited her to Addy's quilting bee, but she didn't feel adequate. Maybe comfortable was a better word. She'd always been shy, and people thought her standoffish. It wasn't something she could change. Lord knew she'd tried.

Life was full of disappointments, it was a lesson ingrained in her. Anytime she had made a friend, they all ended up pulling away, leaving her lonelier than ever. It was best not to get too close. How would she go about finding a place to live? She barely went into town. The trip always made her anxious and edgy. It was easier to just give Cookie a list of things to get at the mercantile.

There was one restaurant in town. In fact, it was newly rebuilt after a fire, and she'd heard nice things about it. The man who owned it, Eats, was a big burly man. She didn't have a choice; she'd have to ask him for a job.

Cinders and Shannon wouldn't put her out, but she couldn't live on their charity. There was nowhere else she could bake and make a bit of money. She hated growing up in the city but now she wished she'd never left. It'd been a huge leap of faith coming west as a mail order bride and it turned out to be a disaster. Imagine a man proposing in a letter, sending money for passage, and then expecting her to be a soiled dove. A shudder went through her.

As she shook her head, her eyes teared. There was

7

nothing to say. That wouldn't be her future, after all. It happened to plenty of women down on their luck. The thought of lying with a man sickened her. There had been little to no privacy in the tenements she had grown up in, and she'd heard her mother suffer more than once. No, she was in no hurry to do any wifely duty. She'd postpone marriage as long as she possibly could.

When was Shannon going to be home? She'd have a solution to her problem, she always did. Ilene's eyes widened; she relied too heavily on Shannon. It was time for her to stand on her own, but how? She should have made a plan a long ago instead of living on Cinders' ranch. People loved her baking, and perhaps she could sell enough to keep herself housed and fed.

A lone tear fell, and she quickly dashed it away. She wouldn't have a place to bake. She'd go and talk to Eats in the morning and see about a job. Clasping her shaking hands she peeked out the window again. Cinders' horse was out front with Tramp's. She waited and waited but they didn't come out. Not a good sign for her.

Shannon might want her to stay. She helped with all the ranch chores. No one could ever say she wasn't a hard worker. Her shoulders slumped as she turned from the window. She had candles to make, and she needed to get them done.

THE WEIGHT on his heart lightened considerably as he talked with Cinders. A full partner, imagine that. He frowned. "You're not doing this whole partner thing to keep me here are you? I haven't earned it."

"Yes you have, or rather you will. You don't have to."

"What?"

"The money I set aside for you is more than enough to buy in, and I really want to breed horses too. The army pays a lot for prime horses. It'll take money to do it."

"Just round up some mustangs. That's free," Tramp suggested.

"Already done that, I need some good quarter horses to breed too. Even saddle broke, mustangs are a bit unpredictable. I know it can be a success. Besides you always liked horses better than cattle."

"You'd want me to take over the horses? It's a good idea, and we have more than enough land on the ranch."

"So, you'll stay?"

"I want my house."

Cinders nodded. "Understandable. I'll need to make arrangements for Ilene. You know, she'd make you a fine wife—"

Tramp raised his hand with his palm facing Cinders. "Wait right there. Every bad decision I've ever made was because of some dang blamed female. No sir, no wife for me."

Cinders smiled. "I think all cowboys think that way at first."

"Well, those yahoos end up changing their minds at the first skirt they see. Not me."

"Makes no never mind to me," Cinders said as he shrugged his shoulders. "You know the last time I saw you, you were escorting Polly, but a few months later Polly returned. I have to say I was surprised you weren't with her. Disappointed too. I'm glad you're back."

"Polly had a banker friend, or so she thought. He tried to get her to marry him. He only wanted her for her money. He stole the money in the bank for himself. Too bad, Polly really liked him."

"That is a shame. I haven't talked to Polly since she's been back. She's never been nice to Shannon, and I don't condone that." He gave Tramp a pointed look.

Heat spread across Tramp's face. He hadn't treated Shannon very nicely either. He was so certain she would cut and run, breaking Cinders' heart. Maybe Shannon was the exception. He'd grown up in a whore house. He'd hated what his mother did with those men. He'd hated her lying cheating ways, and as soon as he was able he had run for it. Luckily, he was only on his own for a month before Cinders' father found him and took him in. Most women couldn't be trusted. It was the plain and simple truth.

He nodded. "I know I haven't been kind to her either. I'll apologize to her and make it right."

"Make what right? Thank goodness you're home, Tramp!" Shannon untied her bonnet, placed it on a wall peg and hurried over.

He widened his eyes as she hugged him. For an awkward minute, he didn't know what to do. Then he hugged her back. Cinders was a lucky man. Shannon too had been tricked into coming to Asherville, Texas as a mail order bride. The saloon owner, John Hardy, had sliced Shannon's face with a knife, scarring her.

Shannon took a step back. "You look good. I'm hoping this isn't just a visit. You are planning to stay aren't you?"

"I have something to say first." He took a deep breath and let it out slowly. "I'm so sorry for treating you so poorly. You never did anything to deserve my contempt. I took every bad experience I'd had with a woman and put it all on you. It was guilt that made me so darn ornery. I took it out on you and told myself I was protecting Cinders. I hope you can accept my apology. I feel as weary as a tomcat walkin' in mud." He put his hands in his pockets and braced himself for a long tirade.

Shannon gave him a sweet smile. "I'm just glad you're

here and in one piece. Of course, I accept your apology." She walked over and gave Cinders a quick kiss. "Olivia is in the wagon with Cookie. Would you mind bringing her inside? Cookie hardly lets me hold her. Who knew he loved babies so much?"

Both men laughed as Cinders walked out the door mumbling something about a baby hog.

"You look real good, Shannon. Being a mother seems to agree with you."

She blushed and then nodded. "We've been blessed." She hurried to the door and took the baby out of Cinders' arms. "Here she is. What do you think?"

Tramp got closer and smiled. "She sure is small. Wow, look at that red hair." Both Cinders and Shannon stared at him as though they were expecting him to say more.

"Don't you want to hold her?" Shannon asked.

Stunned, a sense of panic set in. "I never—"

She took Olivia out of Cinders' arms. "There's nothing to it. Hold out your arms." She set the baby in the crook of his arm and stepped back, leaving him holding the baby. Racking his brain, he tried to come up with something to say. All he could think of was how red and wrinkly she appeared. How this little thing would grow into a beauty he didn't know. Perhaps she wouldn't be pretty. "I think she's wet."

Shannon instantly took the infant into her arms and hurried out of the room.

"You need a wife and children, Tramp."

He shook his head. "That road isn't for me. You enjoy it. I do like the sound of buying in and breeding horses. I relish training horses better than rounding up cattle."

Cinders slapped him on the back. "I'm so glad. Now we just need to figure out where you'll be staying. Jasper is the foreman now, and he has one house that he shares with his wife. Cookie has his own house and that leaves your house, but it's occupied."

"I can stay in the bunk house for a few days until Ilene makes other arrangements."

Cinders frowned looking doubtful. "I'm sure Shannon will get it all figured out."

"Well looky here!" Cookie exclaimed. "You're as unexpected as gunplay in a Bible class. Sure is good to see your ugly face around here again."

Tramp smiled at the older cowboy. Cookie had been at the ranch from the very beginning. "Good to see you too, Cookie."

"'Bout time you got yourself back home where you belong. I would have come to get you myself, but you were in good hands at the Carson ranch."

Tramp's jaw dropped.

"You don't think I'd let you traipse around Texas without me knowin' where you was do ya?"

Cinders laughed. "You never said a word."

"Heck, it wasn't your business. As long as he wasn't in trouble it's best to let a man work things out for himself," Cookie said giving a crisp nod.

Tramp and Cinders exchanged surprised glances, and then they both shrugged their shoulders and grinned.

Olivia began to cry, and Cookie's head whipped around in the direction of the cry. "I'd better go see what's going on. I have a way with the young'uns."

Tramp waited until Cookie was out of sight before he chuckled. "Now that's funny. Does he even know one end of the baby from the other?"

"Not according to Shannon. They'll work it out, I figure. They always do. Damn, it sure is good to see you. Let's ride and I'll show you some of the horses we've been training."

"Sounds good."

ILENE SWUNG up into the saddle and patted the tall, golden mustang. "Nice and slow girl and please don't try rolling onto your back with me on you. It didn't feel good for either of us last time." She took the reins and gave the horse a kick. "Yaw!"

This was her heaven, riding horses. Growing up in New York City, she'd never ridden a horse before. She had been surprised when she'd wandered into the barn and discovered she actually liked the huge animals. They seemed to like her too, and it wasn't long before she had bribed one of the cowboys to teach her to ride. Knowing how to make sweets sure paid off. Now she rode every horse, trained or not. Never near the house, though. Cinders and Jasper would probably have fits.

What they didn't know... She rode for a good while, impressed at how well the horse was doing. It hadn't been broke to ride but she did it. A fine sense of accomplishment washed over her. Turning the mustang, she slowed her to a stop. Riding toward her were Cinders and Tramp. *Oh for goodness sake, I've been found out.*

She'd have to brave it out. Glancing down at the pants she wore, she grimaced. She was a grown woman and could wear whatever she wanted. But suddenly she didn't feel so brave. Men had their own ideas about what was right and wrong.

Cinders was the first to reach her, and he looked more puzzled than mad. Sighing in relief, she then smiled at him.

"I didn't know you rode," Cinders said as he raised one eyebrow.

"I didn't but now I do."

Tramp rode up and whistled. "Great horse. You handle her so well. How long have you had her?"

She wasn't sure what to say.

"That horse wasn't saddle broke a few days ago. Who broke her?" Cinders asked sounding more curious then upset.

"It was me," she admitted reluctantly.

"You? How? When?" Cinders shook his head as he stared at her.

"Lying never gets you anywhere," Tramp said. His eyes narrowed.

"I'm not lying. Gold Dust here is doing much better than yesterday. She's a great horse." Her face grew warmer with each word.

"I guess I don't understand," Cinders said as he jumped down off his horse.

Ilene dismounted as well, Gold Dust didn't like standing around with someone on her, at least so far. She watched Tramp get down, and she couldn't help but admire his long legs and his firm backside. Her face heated.

"I'm really sorry if I broke the rules. I walked into the barn one day, and I was surprised when the horses allowed me to pet them. Then we talked. I learned to ride, and then I found a herd of horses, and they let me ride with them. At first I thought they were running away from me but when I turned, the black horse in the lead turned and followed me." She clasped her hands in front of her and shrugged. Her stomach tightened as a sense of dread went through her. She'd known all along the men would be mad.

Tramp snorted. "How many bones have you broken? I bet you're full of bruises. Who put the saddle on for you?"

She lifted her chin and straightened her shoulders. "None, perhaps and me."

"You saddled the horse?" Tramp looked her up and down.

Wearing pants suddenly made her feel unclothed, but it wasn't practical to wear a dress and ride. "Why do you think that every word that comes out of my mouth is a lie? You don't know me. I'm sorry, Cinders, that you disapprove. I never meant to do something you wouldn't like. I knew the men would balk at me riding the new horses, but I didn't mean no disrespect." She stared at the blades of grass as they danced back and forth with the wind.

"I'm not upset. More surprised. From now on, take someone with you. If you get thrown, you'll need someone to ride for help. I could tell you not to ride the horses, but I'm impressed. I've never seen anything like it. That horse was considered to be the very devil himself. What did you call her? Gold Dust?"

She looked up and nodded.

"Gold Dust is yours to keep." The respect in Cinders' eyes took her by surprise.

She couldn't help the smile that spread over her face. "Thank you. I need to grab Chuck before going back. I usually saddle Chuck, ride out then take that saddle and put it on one of the other horses."

Tramp scowled. "So you saddle twice?"

"Actually it's three times. I have to put the saddle on Chuck again before going back home."

Cinders chuckled. "I'll go grab Chuck, you two ride on back. Where is he?"

"He's under that tree over yonder." She pointed to a big cottonwood in the distance.

"See you back at the ranch," Cinders said before he took off after Chuck.

The ensuing silence was awkward. Tramp's disapproval of her radiated off him. They'd certainly gotten off on the wrong foot.

"Do you need help getting on the horse?" Tramp's voice was full of amusement as he stared at her legs again.

Ignoring him, she mounted Gold Dust and started toward home. If he wasn't Cinders' friend she'd leave him in the dust but good manners prevailed. She slowed her horse to a walk until Tramp caught up.

"Don't you have any fear? Horses can be dangerous, you know. They're not toys."

She turned her head and stared at him. "I never thought of them as toys. Why have you been away from the ranch? Did you fall off a horse and hit your head? It would explain your behavior."

"My behavior?" He shook his head. "You do know that wearing pants isn't a good idea. I can see the outline of your legs, your thighs, and your rear end. You're finely built."

"That is exactly what I mean. How about, it's none of your business. I think you're just threatened a woman can break horses better than you. I wish you luck. Right now I have a few pies to bake." She spurred Gold Dust into a gallop and off they went. She didn't even look back. Whether or not he followed, she didn't care. Toys, indeed. He was a big buffoon.

She slowed the horse when she was just about at the barn. Shannon waved to her and she hopped off the bay and led her to where Shannon stood. "Nice to see you, Shannon."

Shannon smiled. "Did you see Cinders and Tramp out there?"

"Yes, I did. Your husband is the perfect gentleman."

Shannon's eyebrows rose. "So you met Tramp. I have to warn you he's a bit rough around the edges, but he means well."

"Well if staring me up and down is well meaning, it's lost on me. He rubs me the wrong way. He wants his house back, and he wants me to stay away from the horses."

"Is that the horse you were talking about? The mustang that couldn't be ridden?"

Ilene nodded. "Cinders gave him to me. I'm so surprised. At least he appreciates a person who is good with horses."

"Oh my. Tramp was that bad?" Shannon touched Ilene gently on the arm. "You'll grow to like him."

"I wouldn't be so sure of that."

"Things will work out."

"I hope so. It was nice talking with you. I'd better get Gold Dust settled. I have a lot of thinking to do."

"I'll see you at supper."

Ilene nodded and led Gold Dust toward the barn. At first the mare balked at going into the big building but Ilene talked to her, and in she went. She lifted the saddle off with ease, shaking her head at Tramp's doubts that she could saddle a horse. Next she brushed Gold Dust and then gave her food and water. "Get a feel for the stall. I'll put you in the front pasture in a couple hours."

She strolled out of the barn and into her house, intent on making pies but something didn't feel the same. The joy of living in the house had fled as she now thought of the house as Tramp's. Really she was just an intruder, no better than a squatter. Tramp had a right to be mad about it.

Maybe now that she'd be working horses, she'd get a raise in her pay. She could save up and move on. In the meantime, she'd think of something.

CHAPTER TWO

*I*t'd been two days since he'd been back, and Tramp wasn't any closer to getting into his house. In fact, he hadn't seen Ilene except for the evening meals. She wore dresses and he had to admit he missed her pants. The bunk house wasn't bad at all. He'd lived in it before, and he knew almost all the cowboys.

The more he studied the problem, the more he thought he had an answer. Ilene needed a husband and quickly. Then she'd move out and he'd have his house. It should be easy enough. Ilene was very attractive. Her curves were in all the right places, and her dark hair curled wildly and it looked so shiny in the sun. Her face was fair, and her lips always appeared juicy and ripe.

He shook his head, trying to get the image of her out of it. He'd start with the hands, one was bound to want her. Perhaps Rollo would be a good husband for her. He was a decent man. It was about time Rollo married. Now to bring them together.

Tramp spent most of the day working on a plan. The first step would be for Ilene and Rollo to sit together at meals.

There had to be some way for them to spend some time alone. Rollo would realize what a good wife she would make, and Tramp would have his house. So, supper and a walk under the stars it was.

That evening, when everyone started to take a seat at the big dining table, Tramp made sure that there was an empty space between him and Rollo. The other men gave him strange looks as he told everyone where to sit. Tramp just shrugged; it was for the greater good. They just didn't know it yet.

Tramp smiled as Ilene walked to the empty chair. He waited for Rollo to stand and pull the chair out for her but he just sat like a bump on a log. Tramp gritted his teeth and stood. He pulled the chair out, and Ilene nodded her thanks, while Shannon gave him a beaming smile. Damn, he had a feeling Shannon had gotten the wrong idea.

The men were loud and boisterous, and conversation with Ilene was damn near impossible. Finally, everyone was busy shoveling food into their mouths, and Tramp decided Rollo and Ilene needed to get to know each other.

After wiping his mouth with his napkin, Tramp cleared his voice. "Rollo, it really is great that you're still here. You've been here since your daddy died. I admire your commitment to your job. You're a dependable man." He gave Ilene a side-long glance.

"Yep, been here for going on seven years." He went on eating.

"Ilene, isn't that a good trait in a man? Knowing you can count on him?" He felt her stiffen next to him.

"Why yes that is a nice quality in anyone," she answered not looking at him.

This was going to be harder than he thought. He ate some more, wondering what to say next. "You know it's a nice evening. The stars are out. Have you ever taken a walk in the moonlight, Ilene?"

Her face turned bright red. "I most certainly have not. I may be a bit unconventional at times, but I do not walk at night with men."

"I didn't mean it as an insult or anything. It's just that the stars are so bright here. Don't you think so, Rollo?"

Rollo shrugged and continued to eat. This was not going as planned.

"You know, there is nothing scandalous about walking as far as the corral and looking up at the sky. You're still in full view of the house. Tramp, I think it's a wonderful idea for you and Ilene to take a walk after supper." Shannon smiled. "You'll enjoy it, Ilene."

Ilene and Tramp quickly exchanged glances and then looked away.

"I was thinking it would be a nice walk for Ilene and Rollo to take." Maybe it was going to work after all.

Ilene swallowed hard while Rollo practically spit out the water he'd been drinking.

"It is a nice idea, but I'm going to have to bow out. I have guard duty tonight. Sorry, Ilene," Rollo said staring at his plate.

Shannon placed her hand on Cinders'. "Well, since you brought the subject up, Tramp, you can take her."

Cookie put his tin cup down hard on the table. "That's the best idea I've heard in a long time. I'll help Shannon clean up. You two skedaddle."

Stunned, Tramp wondered how the conversation had taken such a wrong turn. He'd seen the stars plenty of times. But he couldn't object without looking the fool. "Ilene, may I have the honor of taking you for a walk?" Her frown took him by surprise. She didn't look one bit happy.

It looked as though she was gritting her teeth. "I'd be

delighted." She stood, grabbed her shawl, and went to wait by the door. "Shall we?"

"Of course." He stood and opened the door for her then grabbed his hat and followed her outside. They walked to the corral in silence.

She looked up at the night sky and smiled. "There are stars, all right. Not much of a moon, though."

He stared at her graceful neck. "There are different phases of the moon."

"Oh, really?"

"Yes, there is a full moon once a month."

"Then what? Does it drop out of the sky making room for a new one?"

"No, the moon doesn't fall." He saw her hand over her mouth and he set his chin. "You're making fun of me."

"Hey, this was your idea. Funny thing, though, I could have sworn you were trying to match me and Rollo together. This walk was meant for me and him wasn't it?" She crossed her arms in front of her and tapped her foot.

He inwardly groaned. "I just figured since you haven't married yet, you needed some help. I was trying to be nice."

Her eyes flashed at him. "Is there something wrong with me? Do you think me unappealing? Let me tell you something, Tramp. I have had plenty of marriage proposals while living here."

"How many? Two? Three? Why didn't you say yes before it was too late?"

Uncrossing her arms she put her hands on her hips and gave him a pointed stare. "Seven proposals you jackass. I'm only eighteen, so I have a few days left before I'm considered to be an old maid."

"Days?"

"Yes, by your judgement not mine. I figured I had a few years left but with your thinking, it's too late..."

Tramp took off his hat and rubbed the back of his neck. "I'm sorry. But you have to agree seven proposals are more than the average amount, yet you turned them all down. Perhaps you want to be an old maid."

"And what's wrong with that? Not every woman wants marriage and all that goes with it. Now, if you'll excuse me, I'm calling it a night." He took a step in her direction. "I can walk myself home. Good night, Tramp."

He watched as she made her way into his house and swore. How the heck did the subject of her being an old maid come up? A man would have to be crazy to allow her to get away. Though she did seem determined about not having a husband. Whoever won her was in for a hard ride.

He went and leaned against the bunkhouse and rolled a smoke. Lighting it he took a deep draw. He spotted Cinders coming across the yard. If Ilene saw through his match-making scheme, he'd bet his horse Cinders did too.

"That was a short walk. You must be rusty where women are concerned."

Tramp chuckled. "Well, I hadn't planned on taking her for a walk."

"I know. You planned for Ilene and Rollo to take that romantic stroll. Shannon wanted me to tell you to either be more subtle or cut it out. She said something about making things awkward."

"I want my house back."

"We'll figure out someplace Ilene can go."

Tramp smiled. "That's what I was trying to do. I was trying to get her married."

"You were a bit obvious. Anyway most of the hands have proposed to her at one time or another. She's a real sweet gal."

"Who else proposed to her?"

"Why? You planning on finding new prospects?" Cinders shook his head.

"I didn't say that."

"You didn't have to. See ya in the morning." Cinders pushed away from the side of the bunkhouse. "You're going to find yourself in hot water one of these days." He walked away muttering about people being in other people's business.

Tramp flicked his cigarette and walked into the bunkhouse. The men had been a bit boisterous before he walked in but now it was quiet as they all stared at him. "What?"

Cookie stepped forward and tilted his head. "I've been elected to talk to you," he said, his lined face serious. "Rollo didn't take kindly to what you were trying to do at the supper table." Cookie shook his head and ran his hand over his white whiskers.

Tramp arched his eyebrow and stared at Rollo. "You couldn't tell me yourself?" Tramp had remembered Rollo as a brave enough man to take care of his own business.

Rollo's blue eyes widened. "It's not that—"

Cookie stepped forward. "We all like Ilene, but we don't want you setting us up on dates with her. You see, this here ranch has become a place for broken hearts. Ilene don't cotton to any of us. Why, Adam over there even brought her flowers. Dill, AJ, and Speed all tried their luck. She sure don't want anything to do with the likes of us cowhands."

A smile spread across Tramp's face, and he chuckled. "None of you? Not one date?"

Cookie's shoulders relaxed as he laughed too. "She won't have any of these knuckleheads. Of course, I haven't tried, I'm sweet on Edith and all."

The rest of the men shuffled a bit then sat down at the large table in the middle of the room.

Tramp put one foot up on a chair and leaned his arm on his knee. "I won't poke my nose where it doesn't belong. I'm desperate. I want my house and you have to admit Ilene is fine of face. I'm sorry I didn't know. I'm sorry I put you on the spot, Rollo. So, how are the girls at Noreen's saloon?" He relaxed as the men one by one grinned.

"The girls are ripe as fresh fruit," Speed remarked. "She even has a couple Mexican ladies that I like. Feels like home."

It was good to see Speed feeling like he belonged. The Mexicans owned Texas not too long ago, and now they were treated with disdain by some of the whites. Speed would be an asset to his horse breeding and training.

"Speed sure sounds like some danged poet," Dill remarked.

Tramp nodded at the youngest of the bunch. Dill had been a new hire, right before Tramp had left. He seemed dependable enough. His walnut toned hair was now tied back, and his brown eyes didn't have the look of wonder a young boy had anymore.

"Well, I'm going to get some shut-eye. I have much to mull over tomorrow. The horses and who to get to marry Ilene."

Usually, eavesdropping wasn't something she did but it couldn't be helped. It was always better to know what the enemy was planning. There was no way she'd fall for one of Tramp's schemes. Who did he think he was? Marrying her off, indeed. Clutching her shawl tighter against her body to ward off the cold, she walked as quietly as possible to her house.

Once inside, she stood in the middle and turned in a slow circle, trying to memorize everything. He was going to rip it all away, and there wasn't a thing she could do about it. She'd figure something out, probably. Her shoulders sagged at the thought of failure. Why couldn't she be as strong as Shannon, or as nice as Addy, Keegan's wife? Even Cecily was pretty, and she knew everything about farming. Ilene was just a poor girl from New York City with no frontier skills. She was learning, but she wouldn't be able to fend for herself.

After lighting a candle, she lifted the candleholder and walked into her room. She placed the candle on a table next to her bed. It threw such beautiful shadows, and she loved watching them. She got ready for bed and slid under the cover before blowing out the candle.

Sleep eluded her and her mind kept wandering back to Tramp's words about marriage, proposals and old maids. Marriage wasn't for her. She'd rarely seen a happy one. Her mother often begged to go back to Ireland, but her Pa had a price on his head and could never return. Her father would remind her mother of the commitment they had both made to fight for Irish freedom. She'd known the risks.

There was always a lot of talk between the men of what they'd done to further the cause and what still needed to be done. A few went back, but many were in her father's shoes. The nights had always started out happy enough. She'd run down to the local tavern and get a pail of beer. It took a lot of practice to get the filled pail up the many stairs. She'd learned pretty fast out of necessity. Her pa's big fist would hit the side of her head if she spilled a drop.

Yes, the men were always jovial until the end of the night, after they drank all the beer. Pa always made her mother cry, and Ilene heard the cries of the other wives as well. No, she refused to live a life like that. Tramp wouldn't change her mind. She'd find somewhere to live.

The next morning, she put her pants on under her skirt, tucked her blouse in and pulled on her boots. She wasn't in the mood to face Tramp, but she'd do it. She'd be making more money as a cowhand.

Squinting against the morning sun she shielded her eyes with her hand. She always helped Shannon with breakfast. It had been a bit of a struggle to be allowed to help. Cookie thought the kitchen was his domain. But lately he'd been spending time with a widow in town. Edith owned the mercantile, and she and Cookie were as opposite as people could be. Since she rarely went to town, she didn't interact with Edith much but she knew Edith didn't like Shannon.

The door to the main house was always open, and everyone was welcome. The smell of coffee filled the air and she couldn't wait for cup. It was usually her private time with Shannon, and Ilene needed her advice. Tramp certainly was behaving high-handed, thinking he could just pawn her off to one of the hands.

Shannon glanced up and smiled. "So, how was your walk last night?" Laughter danced in her eyes.

"Why? Did Tramp say anything about it?"

Shannon shook her head. "No, I was just curious." She touched her scar, something she did often.

Ilene hardly noticed it anymore but Shannon was very self-conscious of it. She refused to listen when people told her it didn't matter. Ilene shuddered at the memory of John Hardy and all she'd been saved from.

She poured herself a cup of coffee and hesitated. She didn't want Shannon to think of her as an eavesdropper, but she needed to confide in someone. "I did hear the men talking last night. I guess Tramp is planning to marry me off. That's why he tried to get Rollo to take me for a walk. He thought we'd be a good match. He doesn't know a thing about me, but he's playing matchmaker. I just don't know. I mean he wants his house. Maybe I could find another place to live."

Shannon placed the skillet on the stove with greater force than necessary. "You're not going anywhere. You're an asset to this ranch. I did hear you're good with horses."

Uncomfortable heat spread across Ilene's face. "You heard about that?"

Shannon laughed. "I wish I'd been there. From what Cinders told me, you have quite a way with the horses. Did you really have pants on?"

Smiling, Ilene nodded. "I figured no one would see me. It's much easier to ride without skirts being in the way." She lowered her voice. "I have them on under my skirt."

Shannon's laughter grew louder.

"What's so funny?" Tramp stood in the doorway, his wide shoulders filling it. He'd shaved, and his jawline was strong, he also had high cheekbones. Oh, he certainly was a handsome one.

Shannon poured a cup of coffee and set it on the table for Tramp. "Just a little girl talk. Did you sleep well?"

Ilene felt him watching her and when she looked up he arched a brow and stared at her. Why couldn't he be nice instead of a spoiled, scheming man.

"Yes, I did," he answered without taking his gaze off Ilene. He turned one of the wooden chairs around and straddled it, taking sips of his coffee while she tried to cook.

She turned her back to him, but she knew he still stared. The bacon started to burn and Shannon had to rescue it.

"Better with horses than cooking? What have you been doing to earn your keep around here?"

Ilene opened her mouth but closed it again. Her life was none of his business.

"Ilene has been a tremendous help to me. She took over all the chores right before and after I gave birth. Speaking of, I hear Olivia stirring." She wiped her hands on a damp cloth and hurried away.

"I know you make candles. What else?"

"Why is it your business what I do?"

"I'm a full partner in this ranch which means I own half of everything. It's my business." He shrugged his shoulder. "But if you don't want to tell me I'll find out anyway."

Putting her hands on her hips, she shook her head. "Really you don't have to concern yourself with me."

"Except when you two are training horses." Cinders' eyes were full of humor as he gazed at Ilene and then Tramp.

A lump formed in her throat. "It's a big ranch. We probably won't run into each other often." She turned away and sliced a loaf of bread. There was no way she'd work with that insufferable— Sharp pain struck her finger, stealing her breath. She had been so lost in thought she'd cut herself. "Ouch." She turned and grabbed a cloth to staunch the bleeding.

Tramp was quick to her side. "Here, let me see," he said in an unusually gentle voice. He took her hand and looked under the cloth. "Did a good job on it, didn't you? Come, let's wash it under the water pump. Hopefully that will stop the bleeding."

She had already thought to do just that. Without a word she snatched her hand back and marched outside. Hearing his footsteps behind her she stiffened.

"I'll pump the water. Hold your hand under the stream."

A refusal hovered on the tip of her tongue, but he didn't seem the type to go away. Ilene unwrapped the cloth from her hand, and then she held her hand under the cool water. She put pressure on the cut with her other hand. After a few minutes, the bleeding stopped. "It's fine now." She waited for him to stop pumping. "Thank you."

"I would have done it for anyone."

"Of course." Funny, how he'd defined their relationship with those words. That was what she'd wanted. Now she was just anyone, and she had the feeling they'd be able to work together. Well, as long as he minded his own business. "I'd best get back to work."

She turned from him but she could feel the heat of his perusal. Did he know she wore pants under her skirt?

TRAMP WIPED his damp forehead with his bandanna and then put his hat back on. He was used to long, hot days in a saddle, but Ilene didn't seem to be faring too well. She had an all over limp look to her. Her shoulders slumped, half of her hair had fallen, and her shirt was plastered to her. In the last half hour, she'd turned an alarming shade of red.

She was a spitfire for sure. Stubborn as the day was long. Worst of all she didn't have enough sense to come in out of the sun. At least her horse had endurance. He didn't see a canteen hanging from her saddle either.

Cursing, he spurred Jack to go toward her. Her body stiffened when their gazes met. He smiled a great big smile. It seemed to bother her. When he caught up to her, she was actually redder than he'd first thought.

She stopped Gold Dust, and the mare danced from side to side as she tried to hold her in position. Her giant frown had to be a big contrast to Tramp's grin.

"Did you even bring water with you?" Dang, his voice sounded gruffer than he meant.

"There are plenty of streams and ponds around." She shrugged her shoulders. "I'm fine."

"You don't look fine. Come on, I'm taking you home." He stared at her, waiting for an answer.

"You're neither my mother, nor my father, and I don't take kindly to orders. Besides, I was on my way to the north pond to cool off."

"There are plenty of watering holes closer to the house."

"Yes, but none with privacy. I go to the north pond because no one else does. I'll look just fine when I'm done." She nodded curtly and rode off.

He held back a string of cuss words and followed her. She was planning to bathe, and he couldn't let her go alone. Somehow he'd have to keep watch without her knowing. Life was fine until it involved a female.

The fact that she didn't turn around to check to see if she was followed had him shaking his head. She wouldn't have spotted him, as he kept to the tree line, but still she should have checked. Did she even carry a gun? He didn't see one, and he knew there wasn't a rifle in the scabbard. Surely, she wasn't that careless.

He turned Jack and rode toward a shortcut to the pond. He wanted to scout it out before she got there. He should have gone in a different direction, but he'd been too curious about where she was headed. He spotted the pond and jumped down. Taking the reins, he quietly made his way toward it. He kept the trees between them for cover and finally found one to settle behind.

The wait wasn't long. Ilene rode her horse right up to the edge of the pond and slid down. Letting the reins dangle, she reached into the saddlebags and grabbed what looked to be clean clothes and some soap. He expected the horse to run but it didn't. Gold Dust stayed right at the pond drinking water and looking around.

Tramp scanned the area again and then turned his attention to Ilene. Dog gone it, she was undressing. He looked longer than was polite before he glanced in the other direction. He should probably turn his back but he didn't want to move and give his position away.

Hearing the ripple of water, he imagined her stepping into the cool water. It was hard not to think of her as naked but he wasn't a saint. After a minute he looked at the pond. Ilene's glorious hair cascaded down her back. She dunked her head and started to soap her hair. He watched her wash and rinse her dark mane.

He turned from her again. If she found out... He sighed and closed his eyes. For some reason he longed to join her. He had to take one more peek. She was getting out of the water, her chemise plastered to her, outlining every curve. He gulped as the water ran off her body. His body reacted as if he was still a schoolboy, and he gritted his teeth.

He was doing the exact thing he wanted to prevent; anyone seeing her. He'd sworn to himself to walk on the right side of things. Maybe he hadn't changed one bit. Maybe he was still the not-so-loyal man who had crossed his best friend. No woman was worth it. He hung his head, remembering how he'd helped Cinders' first wife, Charlotte, step out on him. Blinded by her beauty and promises, he'd covered for her while she met with the then local banker. It turned out to be all false, but it still killed him that he'd done such a lowdown thing.

He'd thought he'd put his guilt behind him but it was still surrounding him. He glanced in Ilene's direction and heaved a sigh of relief. She was dressed and mounting up on Gold Dust. She was amazing. He would have thought she'd need to get on a rock or something to get on the big horse but she pulled herself up in one graceful move. He'd have Shannon talk to her about being safe out here.

He was about to lean back against the tree when his horse whinnied to Gold Dust. His heart dropped when Ilene stared in his direction and saw him. It didn't look good and he wasn't sure there was any explanation that would hold water. He appeared to be spying on her and she didn't look happy as she rode away.

THAT LOW DOWN, mangy, excuse for a man had watched her bathe. She felt filthier than before she went into the water. If this was part of his campaign to get her to leave he'd tangled with the wrong woman. No, she wasn't going to let him get away with such disgusting behavior.

She bet on her sweet mother's grave that she wasn't the first woman he'd scrutinized while she was undressed. Shannon needed to know. But as she pulled Gold Dust to a walk, she wondered if telling Shannon would be a good idea or not. Shannon and Cinders had a good relationship with Tramp. They'd welcomed him home with open arms. No, she needed to be smart about the whole thing. Things could backfire and she'd be the one asked to leave.

Growing up, there hadn't been much privacy but what little they had was respected. Her face grew warm. Tramp had probably seen more of her than anyone else. A shiver went through her body, and she frowned. She wasn't cold or frightened. Was it because she wore pants so he thought her loose? It was hard to imagine Tramp and Cinders being such good friends. They were so different. Cinders was kind and polite.

The barn came into sight, and Goldust went right to it. She swung out of the saddle and walked the horse inside the barn. Two of the men were saddling up. They turned toward her when she walked in but they quickly turned away. Her walk slowed. She'd tried so hard to let each man down gently, and was able to maintain friendships with them all. Tramp was the reason she got the cold shoulder. He'd probably told them one of them had to marry her. He'd invaded every part of her life.

She lifted the saddle off her horse. More often than not, the hands offered to help her. Not today. She carried it to the tack room and put it on the wooden table. Next she grabbed a brush and groomed her horse. "You're beautiful."

"I was going to say the same to you."

Tramp! She spun around and narrowed her eyes at him. "Did you have a nice ride?" she asked. "See anything unusual?" Anger began to bubble up inside her.

He flashed her a grin. "Unusual? No. I did see something lovely, though."

Every muscle in her body tensed. Her mind went blank at his unexpected response. There wouldn't be any witty reply. Taking a deep breath, she let it out slowly trying to calm her hammering heart. Turning back to her horse, she ignored Tramp, but the fact that he was still there made her nervous. She quickly finished grooming Gold Dust and hurried out of the barn.

Perhaps wearing pants wasn't very smart. She saw how Tramp looked at her legs and he probably watched her leave. Her face heated as she briskly walked to her house to get changed. She'd tried so hard to be one of the workers, nothing else. The men all knew their attention wasn't wanted. All except for Tramp, and he was just doing it to get her out of his house.

She changed into a yellow calico dress, checked her hair, and then poured herself a cup of water. Her pies lay out on the big wooden table, ready to be put into crates. Cookie would bring them to town for her. There were twelve in all, and a surge of pride went through her as she gazed at them. She was a hard worker. Maybe she could find a farm of her own. If it was small enough it would be perfect for her. She'd ask Cinders about it later.

TRAMP CUT HIS DAY SHORT. He wanted to be at the main

house when Ilene got there. She fascinated him. He liked her feistiness and the fact it never led to cruel words. He'd been on the other side of such words growing up. If it hadn't been for Cinders' dad, Zed, he probably would have ended up dead by now. He grinned. He'd been hell bent on becoming a gunslinger, but Zed channeled Tramp's pent up energy into cattle and horses.

He probably should apologize to Ilene. She didn't know he was trying to watch out for her. She just thought of him as a letch.

The house smelled heavenly of baked bread and fried potatoes. His stomach rumbled. "Smells mighty good in here, Shannon." He smiled at her as he straddled a chair.

"Takes a lot of cooking to feed all the men, but I've got it down."

"I thought Cookie insisted on helping you."

She chuckled. "That was before he grew smitten with Edith. Now he spends a bit of time in town. He just left, taking Ilene's pies to the mercantile and Eats to sell. Her pies have become very popular. All of her sweets sell." She poured a cup of coffee and put it on the table in front of Tramp.

"Isn't she supposed to earn her keep around here?"

Shannon's brow furrowed. "She does that and more. She helps me with the work, is a wonder with the garden, and Olivia loves her. Now I hear she's going to be helping with the horses. My, she has so many talents."

"If she's so wonderful why isn't she married?"

Shannon shrugged her shoulders. "I'm sure she has her reasons. We grew up in the tenements, the same building actually. My parents were kind, loving people but not everyone was. If you had heard all the begging and screaming each night you'd think twice about hitching yourself to a man too. Her father had a love for drinking. When he wasn't dipping into the pail of beer, he was a nice fellow. But after, he'd turn mean, and Ilene's mother was often forced and beaten. The walls were thin and we were jammed into rooms. It was impossible not to know what was going on."

"I feel bad for her, but I do want my house. I don't want to put her out or anything but it *is* my house." He shook his head. "I need to find a solution." He hadn't realized anyone else was in the house until footsteps came closer.

"I've been thinking the same thing," Ilene said as she put on an apron and dove in to help with supper. "I've got some money saved, and my baked goods are selling. I'm going to try to find a farm of my own."

Tramp practically spit out the coffee he'd just put into his mouth. "Women can't own property."

Ilene put her hands on her hips and gave him a pointed stare. "Where have you been? Women all over the state have petitioned and won the right to own property. I'm not saying people approve or won't give me trouble, but it is possible."

"Married women, I bet."

"Sometimes I think people are just plain ignorant. Don't you know what is going on in your own state? Ex-slaves and, yes, women have petitioned and won the right to own land. Though from what I understand most men aren't happy about it. A widow can own land."

"Of course a widow, but unmarried women? They wouldn't know the first thing about buying property. I bet it's New York you're thinking of."

Ilene pursed her lips and turned away. "We'll see."

Tramp groaned. "Shannon help me out. Explain Texas to her."

Shannon's eyes were filled with mirth. "I do believe she's right. She can buy, but I don't think any man would sell to her. That's just the way of things. Widows get bullied into either remarrying or selling. I haven't seen anyone come to their rescue. Though I've seen plenty of men try to court a widow to get her land."

Ilene's shoulder slumped. "Do you think it'll be so hard?" She looked at Shannon for the answer.

"We're in no hurry to see you go. Isn't that right, Tramp?"

He swallowed hard and nodded. Not only did he have to convince Ilene to leave, he had to convince Shannon it was for the best. He was on his own in this. He'd think of something.

CHAPTER THREE

$\mathcal{T}$he only time Ilene went to town was to attend church. Now she was wondering if she'd have to stop attending. The people were pleasant to her, but she never knew what to say to them. Her social graces were sorely lacking. She smiled and nodded at the right times, but she never felt adequate. It was like being on the outside looking in with such longing that it hurt. To make matters worse, she saw Tramp talking to a variety of men, and by the way they all turned and looked her over, she knew he was trying to find her a husband again.

Her cheeks grew warm, and her heart sped up. How could he? The whole town would think her desperate. Most already wondered why she hadn't married.

After the service she stood in line to greet Pastor Sands. He was a lovely man, who really cared about his flock. Finally, it was her turn, and he took her hand in his.

"It's always a pleasure to see you, my dear. Tramp invited me to dine out at Cinders' place. I wish I could make it. Perhaps another time?" His gaze met hers and held.

"Of course, another time, Pastor Sands. I must hurry

before my ride leaves." Not waiting for an answer, she practically flew down the church steps, only to trip over a tree root. Thankfully she was rescued by Judge Gleason, a town fixture. He was a bit laid back with broad shoulders and white hair that hung past his collar. His face had a very young appearance, and it didn't match his hair at all.

"Whoa, Ilene. What's the hurry?" He held her by the shoulders until she was steady on her feet, and then he let go.

"No hurry. I just wasn't looking where I was going I guess." The warmth of embarrassment flooded her body and all she wanted to do was go home.

"I'd be happy to drive you out to your house. I've been invited to Sunday supper at Cinders' ranch."

Taking a step back, her eyes widened. Right past the judge's left shoulder stood Tramp, who was watching and smiling. Everything within her wanted to go and punch him in the nose. She gathered her wits and smiled. "I'd be honored to ride out with you. Thank you."

"Good, I just sent word to the livery to have my carriage ready. I was hoping you'd say yes. I have to admit I thought you were happy living alone. I had no idea just how lonely you are."

"Lonely?"

"Yes, Tramp told me about hearing you cry yourself to sleep. I've never been married myself, but maybe it's time—"

"It must have been a cat or something Tramp heard. Sometimes I think he's not very smart. I'm not lonely. In fact I've decided not to get married. I want to make my own way." She tried to sound cheerful, but she was aware she'd failed.

"Well, in that case, maybe I shouldn't come to supper."

"Don't be ridiculous. We're having fried chicken, and I'm making a cake for dessert. I'd love for you to come." She stopped talking, afraid she was rambling on.

"May I still escort you, Miss Duffy?"

Ilene put her hand around his offered arm. "It's Ilene. I've never been in a carriage before."

They watched as Simon from the livery drove up in the shiny black buggy pulled by a white horse. "It's lovely!" She smiled.

"I ordered it a while ago thinking I could take it from town to town. I'm the only judge around and once in awhile I get summoned. But it's not sturdy enough for a long ride. Plus Chester rather have me on his back than pull me."

He escorted her to the passenger side and helped her in. He made her feel special in a way she hadn't felt in a very long time. All happiness she'd found lately had been her own doing. Taming the horses, the success of her baking, they made her happy but this was somehow different. It wouldn't lead to anything but she was going to enjoy the feeling while it lasted.

A WIDE SMILE crossed Tramp's face as he watched Ilene get into the buggy with the judge. This plan might just be the one that worked. Judge Gleason was more mature, and maybe that would appeal to Ilene. They could buy land, build a house, get some horses, and have kids. He frowned. He expected to be more excited by the whole thing. He'd get his house back. Still, he didn't feel it.

Perhaps seeing them together and knowing his plan was working would bring on the satisfaction. Living in the bunkhouse hadn't been that bad, but it was the principle of the whole thing. The house had been built for him.

He mounted up on Jack and turned him toward home then waited for Cinders, Shannon, and Olivia to catch up in their wagon. Olivia had been an angel during church. She hadn't cried once. Keegan's little boy, Ryan, who was only days apart in age from Olivia had wailed so loud, his mother, Addy had to take him out of the church. Children had never appealed to Tramp, but he had to admit Olivia was growing on him.

"It was nice of you to invite the judge to supper," Cinders commented as soon as Tramp was riding at his side. He hardly had to take charge of the lines, the horses knew where to go.

"I hope I didn't overstep."

"No not at all. It's your ranch too." Cinders turned and glanced at Shannon. "Right?"

"Of course and we always make extra food. It'll be nice to catch up with Judge Gleason again. He's always been so kind to me." Shannon gave him a reassuring smile. "Why don't you ride up ahead and chat with them."

"I want to give Ilene and Gleason their privacy."

Shannon's eyes narrowed. "You aren't playing matchmaker again are you? Ilene is a bit on the shy side, and strangers make her feel awkward."

"He offered and she said yes. Not much matchmaking there. Besides we'll all be there. Yaw!" Nevertheless, he spurred his horse to go faster. Odd though, she didn't seem awkward or particularly shy. Maybe a bit standoffish, but that's just how she was. He nearly caught up to them but reined Jack in. He didn't want to actually catch up to them. They needed time to get to know one another.

He watched as Judge Gleason set the brake and got out, rounded the buggy and lifted a smiling Ilene down. Did Gleason hold her a bit too long? And what was the great big smile she bestowed on him about? Heck, they hardly knew each other. Doubt swarmed him. He hadn't been around in over a year. He really didn't know much of anything anymore. Hell, even his friend Keegan Quinn had up and got married. Thank God for the men who still lived in the bunkhouse. They were single.

Tramp jumped off his horse when he reached the barn. Adam greeted him and took the horse from him. Adam was another hand who never expected to get married. Tramp ambled toward the house and as he got closer he heard the sweet sound of Ilene's laughter. She really didn't laugh much. Tramp walked into the main house and nodded at the couple. "I guess I'll act as chaperone until Shannon gets here."

Ilene frowned and Judge Gleason gaffed. "I'm old enough to be her father. I don't think a chaperone is required."

"You don't find her attractive?" Tramp wished he could take back his words. It wasn't his business. Plenty of older men married young women.

Judge Gleason cocked his left brow. "What's this all about? Of course Ilene is very lovely. I came to have supper with all of you. When Ilene and I go out it'll be our decision."

Tramp nodded but he felt gut punched. *When?* So he did have intentions after all. Tramp should be happy. It's what he wanted but somehow he didn't like the thought of them together. Ilene had cast some spell over him and he needed the antidote, fast. "Of course. I'm just being overprotective is all. It sounds like the rest are here." Feeling like a fool, he rushed outside.

Shannon resembled an angel as she sat in the wagon with Olivia in her arms. He'd hated her the first time he'd set eyes on her. He really thought she was just another woman after Cinders for his money and his standing in the community. He'd been a fool to have treated her with anything but kindness.

Cinders reached up and took Olivia into his arms, smiling at her little face. Shannon started to climb down herself but Tramp put his hands on her waist and lowered her to the ground.

"Thank you, Tramp. Are the judge and Ilene inside? It was a good idea inviting him. We haven't had him to supper in a long time. It'll be fun catching up." She took Olivia back from Cinders and waltzed inside.

"Still hell-bent on getting Ilene out of your house?" Cinders asked.

"Wouldn't you do the same?"

Cinders pondered for a moment. "Yes, I would. I'm not sure how'd I do it either." He gave Tramp a friendly slap on the back. "We might as well go in."

Tramp still couldn't figure out what was wrong with him. He wasn't jealous. Heck, he didn't even like Ilene. Sure, she was beautiful and spirited. She was good with horses, baked great pies, and people seemed to like her. Everyone but him. He shrugged his shoulders and went inside, to join the lively conversation he could hear spilling through the open door.

Judge Gleason regaled them with stories of cases he'd tried. It seemed to Tramp that criminals weren't the brightest bunch. They all laughed throughout the meal. The only one absent was Cookie. He was spending more and more time with Edith Mathers, the owner of the town mercantile. Personally, Tramp wasn't a big fan of Edith's. She put her nose where it didn't belong, and if she didn't like a person the whole town knew it and why.

Finally Ilene's cake was served. Tramp closed his eyes at the first bite and savored the explosion of sweetness on his tongue. It was heavenly. He opened his eyes to see Ilene's blue gaze boring into him. With a smile, he quickly turned away. He was no good at reading women and he wasn't certain he wanted to know what was behind that stare of hers.

"Ilene, why don't you and Judge Gleason take a little walk?" Shannon suggested. "It's been awhile since he's been out here. I'm sure I can get a few volunteers to help with the dishes." When they hesitated she made a shooing motion with her hands. "Go on the sunshine will do you good."

ILENE SMILED AT SHANNON. "Thank you. I think it's a fine idea, that is if you'd like to, Judge Gleason."

"Burt. My name is Burt," the judge said as he stood.

"Very well, Burt. Shall we?" Ilene asked as she too stood. They walked out the front door into the beautiful sun-filled day.

They walked for a bit, side by side without touching. Ilene frantically tried to find something to say, anything, but nothing came to mind. Story of her life. People must think her simple minded. In a way she was. She didn't know how to flirt or tell great stories. She was positive that anything she did hadn't enough merit for discussion. The judge probably talked to interesting people all the time.

"Nice weather," she commented.

"Yes, yes it is. It's not too hot, and the mosquitoes haven't started to swarm yet."

"I don't enjoy them one bit."

He chuckled. "I don't think anyone does. Unfortunately, between them and the flies, summer can be unbearable. I've known plenty of women who've left Texas for that very reason. However, it's a problem throughout the west. Settlers soon learned not to build their houses close to the ponds and rivers. Between flooding and mosquitoes, they had to rebuild further away. If you travel the state enough you'll notice places with no windows."

They strolled past the barn and reached a stand of trees. She slowed her steps, not wanting to be hidden in the shadows. There were already too many people talking about her. No need to add more fuel. Satisfied they could still be seen from the house, she stopped and gazed at him. "I think you should know something before we walk much more. You're being set up."

His brow furrowed. "Set up? For what?"

"To be my husband. You see, the house I'm living in really belongs to Tramp, and he wants it back and by right it is his. He thinks if he marries me off he can have it. He tried the same thing with Rollo, but what he didn't know is Rollo had already tried to court me. I'm sorry you got dragged into taking me for a walk." She clenched the material of her dress in her hands and let it go. "We may as well go back." Her face heated as her mortification set in.

Burt touched her lightly on the arm. "I'm enjoying our walk. It's not up to them. The only two involved are you and me, and I'd like to walk a bit more. You?"

Relief rushed through her. He certainly was a gentleman. "Yes, thank you." They walked in silence as she once again searched for something to say.

"Relax. Think of me as an old friend. We can talk about the different flowers. Flowers are always good for soothing the nerves. We have many that are native to Texas."

"How'd you know I was nervous?" She glanced at him out of the corner of her eye.

"As a judge I've had to learn to read people. People who come into my courtroom aren't always truthful, and it's up to me to figure it out. After a while it gets easier." He gave her a smile. "Now see that field of blue flowers? Those are Texas blue bonnets. The orange and yellow flowers are Indian paint brushes. There are times when Texas is brown and dried up, and then it puts on a magnificent show like this."

"It is beautiful. I love how you can see from one horizon to the other. In New York I was surrounded by tall buildings. I never saw how beautiful the sunrise could be. We did go up to the roof at times but it wasn't anything like this."

"I love living here. I was born in Texas. We've had our share of wars but we're a tough lot. Takes a hardy person to survive here. And for the record, I think you're as hardy as they come."

Ilene's lips twitched.

"What? Is something funny?" he asked.

She chuckled. "Hardy and sturdy remind me of a big woman able to take on the world. I like to think I'm a bit more feminine than that."

They stopped walking and turned toward each other. "Hardy in a good, sweet, feminine way of course." He reached out and gently pushed a strand of her hair behind her ear. They stared at each other for a moment but the pounding of horse's' hooves interrupted them.

Quickly they each took a step back. Ilene put her hands on her hips are she watched Tramp ride toward them.

"I just wanted to check and make sure you two were fine." He swung down from his horse and stood between Ilene and the judge.

Her eyes grew wide as she shook her head. "The house is still in view. You could have looked out from the front porch of the main house and seen us."

Tramp stared at the ground for a moment, and then looked up. "You were taking so long I thought one of you might have twisted an ankle or something."

The mirth she saw in Burt's eyes had her laughing in no time. "You are an odd one, Tramp."

Tramp shrugged his shoulders and skillfully got them all turned back toward the house while maintaining his position in the middle. He had the horse's reins in his hand the whole time.

"We were talking about Texas flowers, Tramp. Which do you like?" Judge Gleason inquired. His lips twitched as though he was trying not to laugh.

"Flowers? I never gave it much thought. Some are blue, some orange. We have white ones and yellow ones. A flower is a flower I suppose."

"Ilene and I were discussing the names of them." He gestured toward a field of flowers. "Most of the flowers we see here are native to Texas."

"Did you know Ilene trains horses? She even breaks them. She has these pants she wears while riding." Tramp's rushed words made her cringe.

Ilene was tempted to kick Tramp. What was he trying to do? Drive Burt away? Inwardly seething, she bit her tongue and kept in step with the two men. Wait until she got him alone. She'd bite her tongue no longer.

"So, what do you think, Ilene? Do you want to make Texas your home?" Burt asked.

Tramp's eyes grew wide as he turned in her direction. "Were you planning to leave?"

"You'd like that wouldn't you?" She'd had enough of Tramp. She quickened her step until she reached her house, and then she waited. She ignored Tramp and smiled at Burt. "Thank you for a lovely walk. I enjoyed it."

Burt tipped his white hat at her and nodded. "The pleasure was all mine. I'd like to see you again. That is, if you're agreeable."

"I would like that very much."

"Good. Well, good day. I need to get back."

"Good bye."

"Nice to see you, Judge Gleason," Tramp said. He stayed in front of the house, not moving while the judge got into his carriage and drove away.

Ilene crossed her arms in front of her and glared at Tramp. "You insufferable polecat. You go to all the trouble of setting me up and then you intrude on us. Neither was appropriate, nor was it necessary. I don't need you to find men to court me. I don't need you to keep an eye on me, and I don't need you to play chaperone. Have I missed anything or do you understand what I'm saying?" Her voice grew louder with each word but she couldn't help herself.

"I was doing nothing of the sort. Married, unmarried, makes no difference to me. You just need to find a new place to live. Your stubbornness is just going to leave you without a husband. I'm really trying to help. I have your best interests at heart."

She took a step closer and poked his chest with each word. "You only have one thing on your mind and it's you. You, you, you!"

"Is everything alright out here?" Cookie asked as he ambled toward them.

Ilene became aware of her surroundings and instantly grew ashamed of her actions. It seemed as though every person on the ranch was outside staring at them. It was too much. Biting her lip, she lifted her skirts off the ground and ran into her house, closing the door with a firm *thud*. Leaning her back against it, she took a deep breath and tears began to fall.

She'd have to leave. It didn't really matter where she went. What she longed for most, she'd never find; a place of acceptance where she could feel comfortable being herself. Maybe there wasn't such a place for her.

Tramp was a nosey busybody, and right now she wanted to poke him some more. Her finger hurt and she hoped she'd hurt him. Maybe he'd have a few bruises to show for it. One could only hope. Her anger died as she thought of him in pain. He deserved no less.

THE NEXT MORNING, Tramp skipped breakfast and rode out

instead. There'd been a sighting of horses near the north ridge. He rode for a bit before he spotted squatters on his land. He approached slowly, not wanting to get shot. Most that ended up as squatters were in dire straits and at the end of their rope. Their dream of making a good life in Texas hadn't panned out for one reason or another, and they were desperate to provide for their families. He felt for them but he didn't want to encourage such behavior. He'd give them a warning to get off the land.

Just as he'd expected, a rifle was trained on him as he rode closer to the covered wagon. They had set up a camp of sorts. He scanned the area trying to gage how many people he was dealing with. Back in the trees he saw another wagon and groaned.

"Howdy, folks. Stopping for the night?" He hoped they said yes but his hope wasn't high.

An older man stepped out in front of his wagon. "A night, maybe more. Why do you ask?" His voice was gruff but he swayed a bit.

"It's my land. I don't mind a night or two, but anything longer is considered squatting, and I don't cotton that. I've fought for this land. I've worked this land. I'm sure you understand." Tramp had his hand on his side arm.

"Please, mister," a small woman pleaded. She looked deathly white and none to stable either.

"When's the last time you folks ate?"

"A nice woman left us some food a few days ago."

Tramp's blood began to boil. Ilene. It had to be. Ilene had no right to make such decisions. Didn't she know squatters were dangerous? Most times they were sick. Darn her!

"Are any of you sick? I'm including the wagon you have hidden behind the trees."

The man and woman glanced at each other and that was

answer enough for him. "How many people do you have total?"

The man took a wobbly step forward. "We're nine all told. We ran out of food and bullets. So hunting has been hard. We've set traps but not much comes this way it seems."

"Any other sickness I need to know about?"

"No sir. We're just weak and hungry. One woman is having a baby. It's not a sickness mind you, but I'm worried she won't have the strength. Listen, mister we're good God-fearing people. I'm Pastor Joseph Plunkett. I had a church and position all lined up, but the town was burned down when we got there. We'd already left the wagon train and…" He gestured to their surroundings. "Well, here we are." Despite his weakness, he had great inner strength.

"Tell you what. I'm going to get the doctor and some food. If you aren't carrying a sickness, I'll see about getting you folks moved closer to the house. You need to be well to make a new plan."

The woman's eyes teared. "Bless you, Mister. What did you say your name was?"

"I'm Tramp Hart, ma'am. Just call me Tramp. I'll be back in a while." He tipped his hat to her and then turned his horse. "Come on, Jack, we have a job to do."

He rode to town to get the doctor first and to alert the town Sheriff, Shane O'Connor. Sometimes desperate men got itchy trigger fingers. Then he rode for the ranch. Cinders needed to be part of the decision. Why Ilene never said a word was beyond him. She shouldn't have gone near them. Dagnabbit, the woman could have gotten herself in a heap of trouble. Why didn't she use the sense God gave her?

The main house came into sight, and the first person he saw was Ilene. He skirted Jack around her and went on to the house. If he talked to her now, he'd end up saying things he'd regret, so he jumped down and strode into the house.

"Morning, Shannon. How's the little one?" She was the picture of motherhood, rocking Olivia in her arms. Her face was serene, and he'd never seen her look so beautiful before.

"It was a long night. She was fussy most of it." It amazed him how she could smile at him, even after he'd tried to get her out of Cinders' life. He hadn't thought her good enough for his friend. He'd been so wrong.

"Cinders around?"

"He's chopping wood out back. Is something wrong?"

"No, just some squatters. They're near starved and sick. I got the doc to agree to go out there. If they aren't contagious I'd like to move them closer to the homestead for a bit and get them well." He shifted his weight from one foot to the other.

Shannon tilted her head and took his measure. "You know you've changed. Before you'd have sent them on their way, sick or not. I like the change."

His heart warmed at her words. "I'll go find Cinders. See you later." He tipped his hat and left. Helping others did give one a good feeling. He'd never really known that before.

Cinders swung his axe like a man with something on his mind. He stopped when he caught sight of Tramp. "What's going on?"

"Squatters. They're real bad off. I sent the doc out, but I think we should be there to cover him. They seemed nice enough, just down on their luck, but you never know."

Cinders grabbed his shirt and shrugged it on. "Let me get Strike saddled and we can be off."

They walked to the barn, and Tramp waited outside watching Ilene tend the garden. She did do more than her share around the ranch. He needed to curb his tongue around her. He was only making a fool of himself. He hoped she'd look in his direction so he could nod at her, but she acted as though he wasn't even there. It was disheartening, and he wasn't exactly sure why. He still needed to talk to her about the dangers of giving strangers food. He sighed as he heard movement from the barn signaling Cinders was about ready. A talk with Ilene would have to wait.

Soon he and Cinders were riding side by side to the north end of the property. On the way, they intercepted Doctor Martin and Sheriff O'Connor. The four of them continued on until they came to the wagon.

They approached slowly and cautiously. Tramp took the lead. He rode up to the wagon that was in the open and got down. "Howdy folks. I brought the doctor like I said I would."

The old man had his rifle but it seemed too heavy for him to lift.

"What's the law doing here?" the older woman asked, glaring at Tramp.

"I just wanted to be sure Doctor Martin would be safe out here. I don't know you folks. It would be foolhardy to trust you just yet." He gestured to the men on horseback. "This is Cinders. He owns half the ranch. This is Doctor Martin, and the one with his rifle drawn is Sheriff O'Connor. Let's get you folks checked out and then we can go from there."

The couple both nodded. "I'm Pastor Joseph Plunkett, and this is my wife Estelle. We have two other wagons. One has my daughters in it, Ava, Isabelle and Mia. The other one belongs to my brother Peter and his wife Ella. They have two girls, Audrey and Sadie. Like I told Tramp here, the town I was supposed to be pastor of burned down before we got there. We decided to keep going, ended up lost and low on supplies. We stopped here and didn't know what to do. Thank goodness for your gal Ilene for bringing us food."

Cinders turned his head and arched his brow as he looked at Shane. Shane just shrugged. "She never said a word."

Cinders nodded and turned back to the task at hand. "How about we get the doc here busy looking at your family."

Estelle smiled. "That would be real nice. I think we're just mostly weak. Though Audrey and Sadie have a cough. I tried mustard plasters but it didn't work."

"I'll see what I can do," Doc Martin said as he sat the pastor down on a crate.

The pastor kept his eye on the Sheriff the whole time. "You're not going to take us in for trespassing, are you Sheriff?"

Shane O'Connor returned the man's stare. "Not if I can help it."

"You married?" The pastor asked.

"Yes, I have a wife, Cecily. We're newly wed."

The man nodded. "That's a shame. I have three daughters looking for husbands. My nieces too are going to need to find themselves some fine men too."

Shane smiled. "Tramp is single. The rest of us are married."

Both Estelle and Joseph turned their attention to Tramp. "I didn't know you were a single fella. My daughters are a sight to behold," Estelle said with pride.

Shane wanted to groan. They probably resembled wet cats. Besides, marriage wasn't for him.

Doctor Martin went from wagon to wagon and came back. "Nothing contagious. They could use some good food and a lot of rest, though."

"The plan is to take them to the homestead and let them camp there for a while. We have more than enough food. They can plan their next move from there," Cinders said.

The pastor stepped forward. "That is mighty kind of you. I'm wondering if you might drive the wagons for us. I know I can't handle the oxen right now."

Tramp nodded. "Sure. Doc would you mind riding ahead

and asking Ilene and Shannon to have some food ready?" He waited for the Doc to nod before he got on his horse and rode off. "I'll drive your wagon, Pastor," Tramp offered.

Estelle stepped forward. "I think it would be better if you drive my girls' wagon. I think they'd be comfortable with you."

He glanced over at Cinders and then at Shane shaking his head at their knowing smiles. Estelle wanted him to marry one of her girls. Well, there was no help for it now. He needed to get them home. "Let's get going."

CHAPTER FOUR

*A*s soon as she heard the news about the squatters moving to the homestead, Ilene went into her house and made several loaves of bread and cornbread. She'd checked with Shannon to see if she needed help but Cookie was one step ahead of her and took over the kitchen. She put the warm loaves into two baskets and carried the bread and cornbread over to the main house.

"Slice up the bread and divvy up the cornbread," Cookie told her without even turning around. "I'm making my famous stew, but I'm watering it down a bit. They need to eat slow or they'll be sick. Shannon, did you put milk on the table?"

Shannon exchanged an amused look with Ilene. "Yes, you already asked me."

"Did you answer? I would have remembered if you answered. Motherhood can be tricky you know. You think you remember doing something but you never done did it in the first place."

Shannon placed her hands over her mouth to keep from laughing.

"I'm right aren't I, Doc?"

Doctor Martin's eyes widened in surprise. "Well, um, you see. Well, I suppose it's possible." He winked at Shannon.

"So, the milk is on the table?"

Both Shannon and Ilene started laughing.

"I'll check myself," grumbled Cookie. He turned from his stew and checked the table. "Good, milk, bread and butter." He nodded and went back to stirring his pot.

Cookie sure was a character and Ilene envied Shannon's easy going manner with both him and Doctor Martin.

Soon enough the creaky sounds of wagons being driven filled the air. They all hurried outside. Ilene had already met them and it warmed her that Tramp had brought them home. Perhaps he had a good heart after all.

Cinders drove the first wagon, Shane the second, and Tramp the third. Somehow, Tramp had five females with him, all chattering at him, trying to catch his attention. He smiled like a cat who'd just stolen milk from the milking pail.

Ilene's heart squeezed as she watched, and she didn't know why. She didn't care what he did. Except he did say he'd never marry. Maybe he had said it to warn her off. He didn't want to marry her, just her. Most of her joy ebbed away as she watched him lift each girl down. Perhaps there was a bright side. He wouldn't be bothering her anymore. Her heart and head were at odds.

Shannon stepped forward and met each of the guests and made them feel welcome. She didn't seem as self-conscious of the scar on her face when she was on the ranch. It was nice to see. Ilene was happy for her friend.

"Ilene, would you show them to the kitchen?" Shannon asked.

"Of course. Right this way folks." She led them into the house and had them all seated at the table. She wished she'd have taken the initiative to get them inside without having to be told.

Before long, they were all fed. The others, Cinders, Tramp, Cookie, Doctor Martin and Shannon, all chatted and they quickly learned their names. Ilene stood off to the side not knowing what to say and she couldn't tell all the girls apart. Loneliness washed over her as the rest were enjoying themselves. All she could think of was how awkward and backward she was. It wasn't any wonder that Tramp enjoyed them.

She quietly left and went to sit on the front porch. She wanted to be on hand to help clean up. The laughter coming from inside put a lump in her throat. It wasn't that she didn't want to be included. She longed to be a part of it all, but she just couldn't bring herself to join in.

It didn't matter. She'd been like that most of her life, though she'd thought she was used to it. The pain in her heart let her know she wasn't used to it one bit. Her father had often said there was something not right about her and he was right. Everyone else was always at ease while she grew more and more nervous as every minute passed.

Perhaps she was more child than an adult. Her mother had said she'd grow out of it but it hadn't happened.

Tramp came outside and stared at her. Quickly she turned away. He already knew she was a big nothing. A plain girl with nothing to say.

"Are you alright? I know you don't like crowds."

His soft voice eased a bit of her pain. She turned and gazed at him. "I just never know what to say is all. Plus like you said it is crowded."

"Too much squawking if you ask me," he said as he sat in the wooden chair next to her.

"Squawking?" The smile that spread across her face amazed her.

"You know female talk. I don't care about dresses or hair. You can tell they are family, they insult one another. I guess it would be funny but they look at me like a prized bull." He shrugged his right shoulder as he grinned.

"It doesn't flatter you?"

"Oh, there you are!" A pretty dark-haired girl exclaimed as she walked up to them.

"Hi, Ava. I thought I'd grab some fresh air with Ilene." Ava narrowed her blue eyes at Ilene then smiled at Tramp.

"Yes, Ilene was very kind to drop off some food to us. Where is your husband?" Ava asked.

"I'm not married."

"An old maid? I'm sorry I shouldn't have asked. My sisters and I are hoping to find husbands. I think I may have found the one for me." Ava batted her eyelashes at Tramp and blushed.

"If you'll excuse me." Ilene didn't want to see the pity in their eyes. Ava was right she was an old maid. She stood and walked down the steps, across the yard and into her house. She could watch from the window and see when she was needed to clean up. The only problem was watching Tramp and Ava laughing together.

THE NEXT DAY, as soon as breakfast was over, Ilene saddled Gold Dust and rode. It didn't matter where she went. Any place quiet would do. She was all caught up on her orders for baked goods, and she wanted to see if she could find the herd of horses she had spotted the other day. It was almost a shame to catch them. They were so majestic in the wild.

It grew hot, and she was glad Shannon had given her an old cowboy hat to wear. At least her face was shaded. The wind blew the dirt into the air, and she swore every speck had landed on her and stuck. This time she had two canteens and a rifle. Tramp had been right. She hadn't been prepared last time.

She'd ridden west for a spell. She wasn't as familiar with the area, and she hadn't realized how rocky it was. She slowed Gold Dust to a walk and looked for signs of horses. There had been signs of deer traveling this way, but she didn't find any trace of the horses.

She was about to turn toward home when she saw the black stallion. He was powerfully built, and his thick mane blew wildly in the wind. What a sight! He whistled and called to Goldust who began to move despite her objections. "Whoa, girl. Easy now." She pulled the reins hoping to get her under control. It didn't work. Gold Dust reared and unseated her. She flew through the air and landed hard on the rocky terrain. Her horse stopped, and she hoped she might stay put, but after a long look at her, Gold Dust ran in the direction of the stallion.

Stunned, she sat there and watched. The side of her head hurt and when she touched it, she felt the blood. She could feel the blood trail down the side of her face and grew alarmed. She found to her dismay that one of her arms didn't want to work correctly. With one hand she tried to rip the bottom of her shirt to make a bandage but it wouldn't rip. Finally she took her shirt off and ripped out the stitching that connected the sleeve with her teeth. It didn't take long.

She tied the ends of the sleeve together and slowly put it on her head wound. It slipped down and she groaned as she took it off and retied it. This time it was a nice, tight fit. She took the other sleeve off the shirt and made it into a sling for her arm.

Crying out, she put her shirt back on and put her arm into the sling. At least she knew what direction she needed to walk. All she had was her hat and, thankfully, one canteen.

Slowly she stood and realized her left knee hurt, and her right ankle ached. Closing her eyes, she prayed for strength and started to hobble along.

Each step was agony and the throbbing grew worse as she slowly walked. The uneven ground made it difficult, but she was afraid to stop. What if she sat and couldn't get back up? No, she had to go on.

The sun relentlessly beat down on her, causing the fair skin on her arms to burn. The only time she stopped was to take a small sip of water. Her head continued to bleed, and soon the side of her face and neck were smeared with blood as was the front of her shirt.

She stumbled as she limped across the land. How much farther? Flies buzzed around the blood and bit her. No amount of waving and shooing made them leave. What if she didn't make it back? No one would miss her for a while. No one would notice she'd left. Her body screamed for a rest but she trudged on. One step at a time until she was so dizzy, she had no choice but to allow herself to sit down.

On looking back in the direction she had come from, her heart dropped. She hadn't come very far. It seemed so much more. The sun continued to bake her. Texas was so hot, so unforgiving, so hard... so deadly.

Had her life been a waste? She never so much as made a mark on the world. She didn't have a legacy or anything else to show for her time on earth. Only a few friends and a few meager possessions. A very sad existence.

Gold Dust wasn't at fault. She was just being a horse. If anything it was her fault for getting involved with horses when she had limited knowledge of them. No wonder Tramp balked at having her help. She wasn't qualified. She wanted to close her eyes and sleep, but she made herself get back up and continue walking.

Sometimes the pain was so bad tears welled up but she

couldn't afford a good cry. She'd only end up dehydrated. Her mind began to wander. What if she did decide to marry? She'd already turned down most of the single men. The judge was a consideration. He was nice, handsome, and very intelligent. It wouldn't be such a bad match. He seemed like a gentleman, but did he drink? Of course, not all drinkers were hitters, she conceded.

Then there was... Hmm, she'd considered Shane at one point but he never even looked in her direction. He had a nice wife now, Cecily. Would any man gaze at her with the same loving expression Shane had for his wife? Perhaps that would be asking too much.

Sweat poured off her and more flies swarmed. When she was a girl she pictured herself as a mother. She sighed. That meant getting married. It was settled. She'd marry the judge if he was so inclined. Everyone respected him. Where did he live? Did he have a house in town or did he live outside of town? She didn't know much about him at all. Except he did like flowers.

The sun shifted to the west; it had to be after noon. The sling rubbed against her sunburned neck. Then she saw it! Up ahead, grass; glorious, green, lush grass. It lifted her spirits and spurred her on. As soon as her feet were both on the grass, she sat down and rested. It was probably only a couple hours' walk, if she was in great condition. The shape she was in, it would take much longer. But it did give her hope. After taking a swig of water, she got back up and continued her trek.

She walked for at least another hour when she spotted someone on horseback galloping toward her. *Please let it not be a figment of my imagination.* Finally after standing and watching she recognized Tramp. She swayed and everything went black.

WHAT THE HECK? Tramp rode right toward the body on the ground. He was almost certain it was Ilene, but where was her horse? The closer he got the more worried he became. She wasn't moving.

As soon as he was close he jumped down and ran to her. A lump formed in his throat. She was so still. He knelt on the ground beside her and relief so great coursed through him when he saw her still breathing. There was blood everywhere on her, and her blistered skin looked excruciating. Her arm was tied up. She must have hurt it.

Gently, he rolled her onto her back and stroked her sweat and blood drenched hair off her face. "Ilene? Ilene, darlin' can you hear me?"

She murmured but didn't open her eyes.

His heart plummeted. "I need to get you home. I just hope I don't hurt you, getting you there." He lifted her from the ground and laid her over the horse. He then got on the horse as gently as possible. It took a bit of doing, but he turned Ilene enough so she lay cradled in his arms.

He signaled for Jack to walk nice and slow. They were a ways from the house. What the heck was she doing way out here? Gold Dust must have thrown her and from the condition of her skin, she must have been out in the sun all day. He stopped and took off his shirt and covered her with it. The blistering of her skin would cause a world of hurt when she woke up.

Her head wound worried him. Head wounds always bled profusely, but the fact she still hadn't opened her eyes indicated it was bad. He urged Jack into a trot and then finally he spurred him on to go even faster. To hell with the jostling. She needed to see a doctor.

They rode into the yard, and Tramp yelled out for Shannon. Cookie hurried to his side and took Ilene into his arms. Tramp quickly jumped down and took Ilene back into his arms. Cookie led the way into her house and pulled down the covers on her bed.

"Stay with her," Cookie instructed. I'll gather some supplies, send someone for the doc and get Shannon.

Cookie raced for to the door before Tramp had a chance to put Ilene in her bed. Slowly and carefully he placed her on the mattress. He first took the cloth around her head off and examined the wound. It was no longer bleeding, but from the amount of blood on Ilene, it must have bled a lot. Next, he untied the sling she'd made. A pitcher and basin lay on her bedside table. He grabbed a cloth that lay next to them, poured the water from the pitcher into the basin, wet the cloth and then began to cool her burned arms.

He'd seen plenty of sunburn before but nothing like this. The blisters alarmed him. Once he'd done that he took another cloth and began to wash some of the blood off her face and neck. The black flies must have gotten to her too. She was covered in bites. Poor thing.

"What happened?" Shannon asked as she hurried into the room. She didn't wait for an answer. She grabbed the basin filled with now red water and threw the water out the front door. When she came back in the basin was clean. She poured more water into it and took the cleaner of the two cloths from him.

"What happened?" She asked staring at him.

"Heck if I know. I found her on the western part of the ranch. No horse, and by the time I got to her, she'd passed out. She murmured for a moment but hasn't made a sound since. I brought her back here. Cookie went to get the doctor."

"Actually he sent Rollo. He has the faster horse. She looks awful. Look at her beautiful porcelain skin. It's fiery red. I have witch hazel at the house that will help." Shannon sat on the side of the bed and gently bathed her arms. "Have you checked her feet?"

Tramp furrowed his brow. "Her feet? Her boots are still on."

"We don't know how long she walked." She got up and pulled Ilene's boots off. "Just as I thought. Her feet are all blistered too. She won't be doing for herself for the next few weeks."

Ilene moaned and her eyes fluttered open then closed. Finally, she opened them and looked around. The confusion on her face worried Tramp.

"Ilene, you're at your house," he said softly. "I found you out on the range."

She cried out in pain as she tried to move her arm. Gingerly with the other hand she touched the wound at her head. "I made it." Heaving a sigh, she dropped her arm to her side and closed her eyes.

Shannon touched his arm. "It's a good sign that she woke up. I'm just grateful you found her. She seemed to be at loose ends lately."

"What do you mean?"

Shannon walked to the end of the bed and took her time before speaking. "She was happy here. People love her baking and it gave her a sense of pride. She's great at gardening, which came as a surprise to her. And now I hear she's been sweet talking the mustangs. She's so shy, and I thought she was blooming, but instead lately she seemed... I don't know, wilted. I did see her smile when she went for a walk with the judge. I just want her to be happy again."

Tramp nodded then went and grabbed two ladder backed chairs. He carried them into the bedroom and placed one on each side of the bed, holding the back of one until Shannon took a seat. "I'm going to catch a breath of fresh air. I'll be back." He walked out to the front porch, took a cigarette from his shirt pocket along with a match. After striking the match on the bottom of his boot, he lit the cigarette and took a long draw.

He'd hoped to see signs of Doc Martin, but no dust was unsettled for as far as he could see.

Maybe coming home wasn't a good idea after all. Ilene had been happy until he showed up with the exception of her spending time with the judge. His shoulders slumped. He'd thought he'd changed. He'd sworn he'd change his ways. He didn't want to be the cause of any more hurt. At the time he'd made his vow, he'd been thinking about how he betrayed Cinders by driving Charlotte to her trysts. He'd worshipped the ground she walked on and when she chose Cinders over him, the pain never stopped. He'd never forgiven himself for his role in all of it.

Finally, Rollo and Doctor Martin rode in. Tramp's heart leaped into his throat. He hoped the Doc could give them some good news.

"Where is she?" Doc asked as he hustled up the porch steps. He didn't wait for an answer but went right inside, leaving Tramp to follow in his wake. Doc Martin set his bag on a chair next to the bed and shook his head. "What in tarnation happened?"

Tramp stepped into the bedroom. Each time he looked at Ilene, she appeared worse. "I found her out on the range. She was a long ways out, and I have no idea how much she'd walked before I found her. She was still walking when I spotted her, then she went down. As far as I can tell there is something wrong with her left arm, she has that awful gash on her head, and her feet are blistered along with her arms. She did wake for a moment after I got to her."

Doc Martin glanced at Shannon. "Good, glad you've been tending her. I bet there was plenty of blood. Head wounds bleed a lot. He took a glass bottle out of his bag along with a clean cloth. He poured some of the clear liquid onto the cloth and began to dab at the cut on her head. "By the looks of it, it's really not bad. It's not deep, and like you said, she did wake up. We'll have to watch her for a while, but I'm hopeful."

Tramp sighed in relief. Damn, when did Ilene become so important to him? He exchanged hopeful nods with Shannon.

Doctor Martin examined her arm and grimaced when he looked at her sun-blistered skin. "The arm isn't broken but we should wrap it and try to keep her from using it. It's probably sprained. Witch Hazel for her skin would be best. I'll have some delivered to you. I'm sure Edith has some at the mercantile. If you'll excuse us, Tramp, I'm going to have to remove some of Ilene's clothes to check for injuries."

"Sure thing. I'll grab the witch hazel Cookie keeps at the main house." He looked at Ilene for a moment before he left. He was going to give her a tongue lashing as soon as she was up to it. Well, maybe not a lashing, but she was going to hear how her actions had scared the heck out of him. He walked out of the house and across the yard rubbing the back of his neck. As he grabbed the bottle he needed and headed back, he realized that telling her he was scared wouldn't do. He didn't want to seem like a sap. He was good at acting indifferent. Indifferent would be good.

He waited in the kitchen until Shannon opened the bedroom door. "Well?"

Shannon stepped out and smiled. "It's not as bad as it looks. Her ankle is swollen, so Doc Martin wrapped it up. She'll mend. I need you to stay here with her. Olivia is with Jasper's wife, Marie, and she needs feeding."

Before he could say a word, she was out the door. His jaw

dropped. He was supposed to stay with Ilene? He scratched his chin as he shook his head.

"Well, good I'm glad you're back. Sounds like you're moving in for a spell." Doc Martin put his bag on the table and took out a brown bottle. "This is laudanum. It's for pain. Too much can be disastrous. Just six drops in water twice a day. I'll be by tomorrow to see if that is enough. Oh, and she's awake now. Use a cloth and put the witch hazel on it and pat it on her skin. Don't rub it on, her skin is in bad enough shape, but she'll heal." He picked up his bag and shook Tramp's hand. "I'm glad she's in good hands."

Tramp nodded. His heart began to race. What did they mean he was taking care of her? Certainly Jasper's wife or maybe Shannon and the baby could move in for a while. Sweat formed on his brow. He wasn't good with sick people, not that he'd been around many but surely he wasn't. Coffee, he needed coffee. He stoked up the cook stove and put the coffee on to boil. He couldn't stall any longer.

He put a smile on his face and walked into the bedroom. One of the things he'd wanted when he had drawn up the plans for the house was windows in all the rooms. Many houses had only one or two windows. That was to keep the heat inside and the bugs out. He wanted his house full of light. He planned his with glass windows and he smiled at the sun shining across the bed, Ilene lay in.

She was in her chemise, and the covers were definitely not on her. Someone, probably Shannon, had wipe most of the blood from her hair. Good Lord her calves and feet were exposed. One ankle was bandaged. What a contrast, her legs were so white while her arms were so red. She cleared her throat, and he moved his gaze from her body to her face. "Hello," he said in a soft tone.

"Hello yourself," she croaked out.

"I, well, I thought you'd have more clothes on or at least have a sheet covering you."

"It hurts when the sheet is on my arms. You could probably pull the sheet up to my waist but could you wait a bit? I'm feeling so hot." A lone tear trailed down her face. "Thank you for finding me."

"I'm just glad I did. No one is out that way often. I was looking for mustangs." He pulled the chair back a bit more from the bed before he sat down. "It surprised me as all get out to see you there—and on foot."

"I saw the black stallion, so you were on the right track. He whistled and off Gold Dust went, leaving me on the ground." She squeezed her eyes closed then opened them. "The pain is unlike anything I've ever felt. Doctor Martin gave me some medicine and I'm hoping it will work right soon."

"It will, just hold on. I figured Gold Dust threw you. You must have walked a long ways."

"Yes, a few hours at least. I had my canteen on me." She tried to smile but it quickly turned into a frown. "Even my face hurts. Shannon said you're going to take care of me."

Now was the time to back out and put an end to the assumption he'd play nurse to this woman. He had more important things to do. Looking into her eyes, he couldn't tell her she was wrong. "Yes, I hope that's fine with you. If you'd rather I find a woman to help you, I can."

"No, Shannon explained to me that she would take care of anything I need privacy for and since it's a family ranch it's not improper. I'm a bit fuzzy on the last part. I would have thought it would be thought of as outrageous behavior."

"A family ranch means no one talks about what goes on at the ranch. We're family." A lump formed in his throat at the word *family*. It was really all he'd longed for his whole life, a real family. It never occurred to him that he already had one and more. To think he had thrown it all away for all those months. It humbled him. "Do you need anything?"

"No, I'm just so sleepy."

He sat there watching over her long after her eyes closed and her breathing became deep and even. Somehow, she made him feel comfortable in his own skin again. Being with her brought a sense of peace. Finally, he shrugged, stood up and went into the kitchen for a cup of coffee.

It was a big responsibility, taking care of someone. He'd only taken care of animals. He wasn't qualified, and he had no business tending to a woman. What did he even know about her? She liked to bake and was making money at it. She had some uncanny way with horses, well not today but she was amazing. She pulled her weight around the ranch. Independent and capable came to mind. She didn't seem to like people except for Judge Gleason. What else? She hailed from New York City. For a city gal, she had sure grown accustomed to ranch life fast. Her hair was nice—actually more than nice—and her blue eyes sparked at him when they talked.

He sat down, put his elbows on the table, and set his head in his hands then groaned. He knew more about her than most people he'd known forever. There was no sense in trying to get out of it. It would only make him look bad. No, he was in it until she was better.

CHAPTER FIVE

*I*lene opened her eyes and blinked a few times. The flame from the oil lamp on the table next to her threw dancing shadows above her. She took a deep breath and winced. Her whole body hurt from her head to her toes. Turning her head was torture, but a slight smile tugged at her lips when she saw Tramp folded into the chair with his head tilted to one side, asleep.

His hair was mussed, and he looked much younger, almost as though he was finally peaceful inside. He still had deep lines from working outside all the time but the serious-ness he always carried faded. He must have a lot bottled up inside of him.

Her arms hurt and were so hot that she was surprised when she shivered. Was Gold Dust all right? It wasn't good for a saddled horse to be out in the wild. The tack could get caught. She needed to find the mare and unsaddle her. She tried to lift her head and realized she wasn't going anywhere. Good Lord, what was she doing with just her chemise on and Tramp in her bedroom? She groaned.

Tramp sat straight up. "Are you in pain? Where does it hurt?"

"Yes and everywhere. What are you doing here?"

"I'm taking care of you." He stood and raised his arms up over his head, stretching.

"Why you? Why are you in my bedroom? Tramp, what is going on? Did you undress me?" Her voice grew louder with each question.

"Do you need more laudanum?"

"No, I don't. Can you at least help cover me up? Then you can go." His amused stare infuriated her. She started to clench her fists and realized one of her wrists was bandaged. Closing her eyes, she took a deep breath. "How hurt am I?"

"Oh, darlin' you'll live. I know it doesn't look good. You sprained your wrist and one ankle. Doc Martin thinks your knee looks very swollen. You hit your head and it bled—a lot. You're sunburned as all get out. Oh, and you have blisters on your feet." He sat back down. "Shannon volunteered me to stay with you. She undressed you, and you have two under-dresses on, so I can't see through them or anything. I wanted to cover you, but with the burns and all, it hurt you."

"So, you're not trying to take advantage of me?" She smiled when his eyes grew wide. "I'm joking. I'm grateful you're here. Is Shannon going to be here in the morning?"

"I have no idea. It sounded to me that I'm your caretaker. Don't worry about it. Don't you remember our conversation when you woke up earlier? I told you about this being a family ranch."

She furrowed her brow for a moment then nodded. "I do remember. It's a bit hazy though. What about the girls? You know the squatters. Surely one of them could watch me." Tramp's brows raised, and she couldn't tell if he thought it a good idea or if he didn't want to be replaced. What was she thinking? Of course he didn't want to be here.

"I can talk to Shannon about it. I think they have their own to look after. They were thinner than they looked at first. From what I heard, it's going to take them a good while to regain their strength."

"Those poor people. Thank you for bringing them here. I thought for sure if I told you about them, you'd have them driven off the ranch."

He glanced down at his boots as though he found them to be fascinating. "Truthfully I did intend to run them off. It's just the way of things out here. You can claim land as yours but you need to make sure it stays yours. There is a lot of land in Texas. Enough for everyone to have their own. I don't see a reason to try to make your home on someone else's property. I suppose there are always exceptions."

"Ava seems taken with you." She didn't know why his answer was so important to her but it was.

He glanced up at her. "I suppose so." He gave her a big smile and her heart dropped. "You looked pained. Let me get the laudanum."

"No! I don't want that nasty stuff anywhere near me. You take it when you're ill, but some people can't stop taking it, and they lie and steal to get more."

"Not if you only take it when you're sick."

She cried out as she shook her head. "I just don't want it. Promise me you won't try to put it in my coffee or something. I've seen what it can do, and I want no part of it."

He reached out and touched her hair. "Don't worry. I might be a big pain but I wouldn't do something so underhanded. I won't give you any more."

Sighing deeply she then yawned. She could feel exhaustion take over. "Thank you, Tramp." She closed her eyes.

It had been three days of taking care of Ilene, and Tramp was at the end of his tether. Not that she was demanding or unreasonable. He just itched to go out and round up horses. He was made for doing, not sitting. Cookie brought over the meals and took their laundry. Doctor b stopped in to change her bandages. That morning he'd shown Tramp how to wrap her ankle and wrist. Shannon was a frequent visitor, and she always brought Olivia. It surprised him how much he'd come to dote on the baby.

She didn't seem to have any other friends. Her sadness when he asked about friends pulled at his heart mighty fiercely. Ava Plunkett came in a few times, but he could tell the visits were to see him more than out of concern for Ilene.

Ilene never smiled at Ava. In fact, she acted as though she couldn't wait for the other woman to leave. She either answered Ava's questions briskly or not at all. It was all he could do not to laugh.

At the soft knock on the door, Tramp groaned inwardly, hoping it wasn't Ava. He walked from the kitchen to the front door and opened it. It was a surprise to see both Judge Gleason and Edith Mathers. Damn, so much for having just the family know he was here with Ilene. He mustered up a smile and gestured them inside. Before he closed the door he scanned the yard for Shannon or Cookie. Only the Plunkett family was about. He closed the door and followed the two visitors into the kitchen.

"This is a nice house," Judge Gleason said as he touched the walls, examining the workmanship. "You designed this didn't you?"

Tramp smiled and nodded. "I did with Cinders' help. It did turn out well, didn't it?" His smile faded when he noticed Edith's glare. "Well, I'm sure you're here to see Ilene. Let me make sure she's decent."

Edith gasped and put her hand to her chest.

Damn, he'd said the wrong thing, the worst thing. He hurried to the bedroom and inwardly groaned. Ilene was sleeping. He hastily grabbed the sheet and began to put it over her when he heard another of Edith's gasps. He dropped the sheet; it wasn't worth making Ilene uncomfortable to make Edith happy. The damage was already done.

He glanced at Edith and then at Judge Gleason who entered the room behind her. He could only imagine what the speculative looks they gave him meant. "She's asleep. Why don't we talk in the kitchen?" He sighed as they all walked out in single file. "Would you care for something to drink?"

Neither answered; they just stared at him, and a lump formed in his throat. He'd heard about shotgun weddings, and he had a sinking feeling he was to play the groom in one.

"Does Cookie know you're here? I can't imagine him condoning something like this. Shannon has always gone against propriety, but Cookie? Are you even supposed to be in here? Did you sneak in so you could take advantage of Ilene?"

It was on the tip of his tongue to say yes, he had snuck in but they had interrupted his evil intentions. "Everyone knows. Nothing has been going on. I've been taking care of her. She can't do for herself, and everyone else is busy. I'm the one who found her out on the range."

Judge Gleason rubbed the back of his neck and began to pace. "This type of thing destroys reputations. Why I made Cinders marry Shannon when he wanted to hire her. You know, out here your good name and your reputation is all you've got. This whole thing stinks bad. Other arrangements could have been made. We met the Plunkett family. There are more than enough of them to share in taking care of one woman."

Tramp widened his eyes. He thought the judge would

have been on his side. "This is a family ranch. We do for each other, and no one finds out."

Edith laughed. "Who are you trying to fool? When has one secret ever been kept in all of Asherville? Nice try, though. So, are you going to marry her?" She crossed her arms in front of her and tapped her toe.

Judge Gleason nodded. "I agree the sooner the better. Dang, Tramp, why did you have to go and ruin Ilene? I was getting ready to court her."

"I'm—I'm not ruined." Ilene barely got the words out before she began to sway.

Tramp raced to her side, swept her up into his arms and carried her back to bed. "Hey, darlin', don't you worry now. You just concentrate on getting well."

"No, they are trying to make something out of nothing." Tears formed in her eyes.

"I'll take care of it. You can count on me. Just rest for a while. I'll be right back." He turned to leave the room and right outside the doorway stood Edith and Judge Gleason. He wished he could just push them out of the way and leave the house. But he couldn't. Wouldn't. No more running away.

"I'd like to speak to you both outside." He walked to the door and glanced back at them to make sure they were following. He saw them exchange glances, and after a few breaths they followed. He waited until he shut the front door before he spoke. "Listen, I don't know what you two are trying to pull but Ilene is sick and injured. The last thing she needs is you two stirring up trouble."

Edith took a step toward him. "You know very well you are in the wrong. You are going to marry that girl."

"I'm sorry he can't. He's already marrying me." Ava Plunkett sidled up next to Tramp and put her hand on his arm. "Thank you for watching Ilene for me so I could wash up. I'll just head on in now." She gave him a slow smile before she went into the house.

Tramp stared at her retreating form. What the heck had just happened? Maybe she thought she was helping but there was no way he was going to marry Ava. He wasn't marrying anyone. He turned back to his two guests and didn't rightly know what to say. Edith had a big scowl on her face while the judge had his right brow cocked.

Tramp shifted his weight from one foot to the other, trying to figure out what to do. Going with Ava's lie would be the easiest but he didn't want any more lies in his life. "I never asked Ava to marry me."

Edith's jaw dropped and then she snapped it closed. "You can't trifle with women and not have them expect marriage. Just how many women have you been using this way, Tramp? I have to tell you I'm highly disappointed in you. Does poor Ilene know about your trysts? Poor, Poor Ilene."

Poor Ilene? His head felt the urge to start spinning. "Listen, Edith, nothing has been going on and now that I think of it, it's not any of your business. Like I said this is a family ranch which you are no part of." He was instantly sorry for his last few words when he saw the hurt on Edith's face. "Talk to Cookie and have him explain. I have things to do."

Judge Gleason took a step forward. "Now you wait one minute. Something underhanded is going on around here, and you've got Ilene mixed up in it. What do you have to say for yourself, and how are you planning to make things right?" His voice grew louder with each word. The whole Plunkett family turned and stared.

Tramp put on his mask of indifference. It was harder to wear this time. He wanted them to know he was angry, but that wouldn't help Ilene any. "The only thing going on is Ilene nearly died out on the range, and I'm nursing her back to health. Right now I'm the best candidate. The other men are needed to round up the cattle, Shannon is busy with Olivia, Cookie and Jasper's wife are doing the rest of the work. Cookie brings us food. Shannon comes and takes care of any of Ilene's personal needs, including bathing her. Mainly, I watch over her as she sleeps, and I make sure she eats. I even read to her. But that is all. Did you even look at her? She can hardly move, so how we could be doing anything inappropriate is beyond me. I think of it as one friend looking after another. That is all I'm going to say on the subject. Now I need to go, Ilene isn't so fond of Ava. Good day." He didn't wait for their replies, just turned and marched into the house and slammed the door shut.

He didn't care about the shock on their faces or their disapproval. None of it mattered to him. Now he had to untangle the mess Ava had made. He stopped and took a deep breath. She was just trying to help. She didn't need his anger.

ILENE LISTENED while Ava chattered on and on about marrying Tramp. It was painful to hear, but Tramp had his own life. He'd never mentioned Ava to her, so the news stunned her. A lump grew in her throat.

"He is ever so handsome, don't you think?" Ava asked as she plopped herself down on a chair next to the bed.

"I suppose."

"He has wonderful manners, and have you noticed how strong he looks?" Ava smiled widely.

"He is strong. He's had to carry me more than once." Ilene was being catty but she didn't care. "I'm getting a bit tired. Could you go make a fresh pot of coffee?"

Ava nodded and stood. "Of course. I'm good in the

kitchen. I'll be a fine wife." She walked out of the room with a bounce in her step.

Ilene's bottom lip trembled as she tried to fight off the despair that filled her. She had no claim on Tramp. He probably didn't really like her. Why would he? She was just someone he was helping out at the instruction of Shannon. He must be visiting Ava whenever Ilene napped or was with Shannon. She tried to fight off the despair that filled her.

It was none of her business. Tramp was his own man and could marry whoever he wanted. And then…Tramp and Ava would be living in this fine house. Ilene sighed. She'd known she'd have to leave soon but it felt as though she was being pushed out. When was the wedding taking place? Was Shannon helping them to plan it? Each thought squeezed her heart. There must be something special about Ava. She'd only been here a few days.

Ilene lay looking at the ceiling willing her tears to go away, but instead they slid down the side of her face. She heard Tramp come back into the house and then she heard him and Ava murmuring. Her tears spilled faster.

"Here's your coffee, Ilene." Tramp put the cup on the table and frowned. "Hey, is the pain that bad?"

Ilene didn't trust her voice so she gave him a slight nod. The pain of her body was nothing compared to the pain in her heart. There was no way she'd ever let him know. She'd been a fool to get attached to him.

"Perhaps some coffee will help?" He sounded doubtful but he smiled when she nodded. He helped her into a sitting position and fixed her pillows behind her back before he handed her the cup.

"Thank you," she said, her voice sounding scratchy. She took the cup and took a sip. Who could make coffee this bad? She took another sip trying to figure out where Ava had gone wrong. After a third sip, she knew and her eye widened as she stared at Tramp.

"I told you no laudanum. I thought I made myself clear. How could you? Do you want me asleep and out of your way so badly?" She shoved the cup at him, splashing coffee on his shirt.

Tramp frowned and then first smelled the contents of the cup then he tasted it. A look of fury crossed his face. "It wasn't me, darlin'. I'll be right back." He shook his head as he left.

He seemed to be surprised. It must have been Ava. She didn't know, maybe she was trying to help. It was so hard to figure out what was going on from inside the bedroom. All she could hear was more murmuring and it made her whole body tense wondering what was being said. She heard the front door close and turned her head, watching the bedroom door to see who was still in the house. She sighed in relief that it was Tramp.

He turned the chair around and straddled it, crossing his arms on top of it to rest his chin. He smiled. "You don't have to worry about Ava again. She didn't know you didn't want the drug. She should have asked though."

"Yes she should have. I could have taken some already and it would have been a double dose. It's not something to be so lackadaisical about. As soon as I'm healed up, I'll move out of your house." Her gaze met his and held. He didn't appear to be a happy husband to be. There was deep sadness in his eyes.

Tramp pressed his lips together and paused before he spoke. "Edith and Judge Gleason came by to see you and when they saw me their reaction was worse than seeing a nun in a whore house." A slight smile crossed his face. "Edith got her back up, and Gleason thought I was taking advantage of you."

"Did they see how bad off I am? There's nothing going on."

"I know. They suggested I marry you, and I took them outside to talk so we wouldn't wake you and upset you. I think I got it all straightened out."

"Well, thank you." Why didn't he just come out and tell her about his impending marriage to Ava? It wasn't her business. Darn, her heart ached again. "I'm really sleepy now."

Tramp stood. "Sweet dreams." He took the coffee cup away with him when he left.

TRAMP SAT on the settee in the front room; his legs stretched out in front of him, and gazed out the window. The Plunkett family sure was a tight-knit group. The stronger ones helped the weaker ones walk to regain their strength. They were usually talking and laughing. What he wouldn't give to be part of something like that. But no. He shook his head. He wasn't willing to marry to be part of the group.

Would he ever have his own family? He hadn't thought he wanted one so badly. He'd had such an empty hole inside of him for so long, and now that he knew the cause he wanted to fix it but not by marrying someone he didn't love.

At least Edith and Judge Gleason would stay out of his business now. He didn't like lies, but once in a while there was no avoiding them. He was surprised to see Cinders hurrying across the yard toward him. Tramp got up and opened the door.

They shook hands and Cinders gestured with a nod of his head he wanted to talk outside. Tramp stepped outside and closed the door quietly, anxious to hear what Cinders had to say. "Is something wrong with the ranch?"

Cinders took off his hat and slapped it against his thigh.

"Not with the ranch, but I certainly got an earful from Edith. You know how she is. She wants you and Ava to have your wedding as soon as possible. This way Ilene will have a clear name."

Tramp stared at his friend. "I'm not marrying Ava. Ava told them I was, but I never proposed."

"Did you tell Edith or the judge you weren't getting married?"

"No. They were planning a shotgun wedding for me and Ilene, and I wasn't going to allow it. There is nothing improper going on. They have no right telling me what to do." His voice began to rise.

"Listen I know how you feel. I had to marry Shannon. Best thing that ever happened to me. I really think we need to get it all straightened out. Joseph Plunkett thinks you're marrying his daughter and soon. He wanted to know when Ilene was moving out of the house so they could move in."

"They?"

Cinders sighed. "They are a close family, I was told."

"I'm going to go and talk to Ava and her father. I never proposed. Heck, I don't think we've ever done more than greet each other in passing. This has gone far enough. I just wanted to spare Ilene the accusations those two were making." He rubbed the back of his neck as he scowled.

Cinders nodded. "It's unfortunate they came by. Gleason wanted to court Ilene, and Edith wanted to surprise Cookie. I wonder who she has minding the store." Cinders shifted his weight from one foot to the other. "There's something else. I'm sorry as can be Shannon put you in such a predicament. I don't want to get into your business, but have you considered marrying Ilene?"

Tramp stared at his friend. "Marry Ilene? Are you loco?" He heard a gasp and turned toward the house. Ilene stood in the doorway with her hand over her mouth and her eyes wide. "Ilene—"

"I was looking to see if Shannon was around to give me a hand." She swayed and Tramp raced to her side.

He picked her up and kicked the door closed with his foot. "I'm sure Cinders is on his way to get Shannon now. You shouldn't be trying to walk. You could injure yourself worse. Here, let's get you back into bed." He bent down and placed her on the mattress. Her hair smelled of lavender, and it surprised him that he'd never noticed before. He took a step back, wracking his brain for something sensible to say. "I'm sorry about what you heard out there."

She waved her hand dismissively. "Don't give it another thought. Don't worry about me." A ghost of a smile lifted her lips.

"Is there something I can do for you or do you really need Shannon. I don't mind getting the chamber pot out for you."

She turned a bright shade of red. "No it's not that. It's just something women go through."

He drew his brows together and tilted his head while he stared at her. She turned even redder. Suddenly it occurred to him. Dang, he heard women were demons when they got their monthlies. He felt his face heat. "I'll go see what's keeping her."

He left the room and leaned against the wall next to the open door. Now what? He didn't know what to do for her, and he certainly didn't want to see her demon side. He wiped the sweat off his brow with his shirt sleeve. He'd have to ask Cookie for some whiskey. It might be the only way he'd survive.

Shannon hurried in, and her mouth dropped when she spotted Tramp. "What happened? Do we need the doctor?"

"No, it's a women thing." He did *not* want to have this conversation.

85

Shannon smiled and nodded. "I'll take care of it." She sailed into the bedroom and closed the door. A few minutes later she left only to quickly return with a basket. "Ilene has probably enough of her own supplies but I'm leaving extras."

Tramp groaned and ran his hand down his face. Two bottles of whiskey that was what he needed. Cinders would know how to survive, but he couldn't embarrass Ilene by asking Cinders. He took a deep breath and decided to make coffee. Coffee always helped. Didn't it? His shoulders slumped. What did he really know about taking care of anyone? He wasn't qualified. Maybe he could get Ava to stay with Ilene.

Shannon came out and nodded to him. He was so tempted to ask her to have Cookie get him the whiskey, but he thought better of it. He didn't want Shannon to know about the demon qualities of women. She probably knew but it wouldn't be right to acknowledge it.

"Are you going to be all right? You look a bit green." Shannon gave his arm a quick squeeze. "You need to rest."

He nodded. "I will thank you." He watched her leave and contemplated what to do next. Should he check on Ilene? Should he let her be? His whole body was wound so tight he needed to get on his horse, rope a steer, and wrestle it to the ground. He longed to be outside, but instead he was stuck in the house.

He heard a groan from the next room and he nearly groaned himself. There was nothing for it he'd have to go into the bedroom. He walked in and was surprised to see Ilene sitting up on the bed with a smile on her face. Was this some kind of test or some kind of joke? Why was she smiling at him? Something wasn't quite right. "Did you need something?"

Ilene shook her head. "I'm fine, really I am. I'm getting

better every day, and I plan to be out of here very soon." She smiled at him again, causing him to frown.

Tramp felt a blush cover his face. "I meant, um, I meant do you need anything for your special problem?" He rubbed the back of his neck as he quickly looked away from her. It was very quiet for a few moments, and he snuck a peek at her. Her face had turned a brilliant shade of scarlet.

"You don't have to worry about that. Shannon took care of everything. Why don't you go outside and get some fresh air for a while? I'll be fine here alone." He hesitated, and she shook her head. "Go on, it's not right for you to have to spend all your time here with me."

He studied her for a moment and then nodded. It might do him good to get outside for a while. He turned to walk out the door and suddenly stopped. Was this the time the demon would appear? He waited for a moment expecting her to change her mind, but it didn't happen. He wandered into the kitchen and stood there for a few moments just to be sure that she didn't need him. All was silent. Shrugging his shoulders he went out the front door.

The first person he saw was Cookie, who actually scowled at him. Cookie could be ornery at times, but this scowl was directed right at Tramp. He walked closer to the corral, where Cookie was watching Rollo try to break a horse. Rollo looked like a rag doll being tossed back and forth as he rode the bucking horse.

Tramp stood next to Cookie, leaned his arms on the top rail of the corral and then turned his head, staring at Cookie. "Mind telling me what that look is for?"

"I had to go ten rounds with Edith trying to defend you. I'm not entirely sure you're worth defending but Ilene is. Just so you know her name has already been dragged through the mud in town." Cookie turned until his body faced Tramp.

"You best do right by that little gal." Cookie shook his head and walked away.

Things were much worse than he imagined. Damn, it looked like he was going to be forced to marry Ilene after all. He should have protested more when Shannon suggested he take care of the injured woman. He should have put his foot down. He should have... He couldn't think of what else he should have done, but he was sure there was something he'd left out. He'd hardly been back any time at all, and already people were planning for him to get hitched.

Perhaps if he spent time with Ilene in a normal fashion he'd come to like her. She was pretty, and she could cook. It was just that being forced to do something stuck in his craw. He took a deep breath and shrugged. Well, no one was making him do anything right now. There might be hope yet. Maybe one of the men who had already asked her would be available to marry her. He'd think on it; there was bound to be someone. People called him stubborn and they'd be right.

CHAPTER SIX

*J*lene sat up in bed taking stock of her injuries. She wiggled her toes then made a circle with her foot to test her ankle. A twinge in her ankle brought on a wince, but it wasn't even half as bad as it had been. Gingerly, she bent her legs, and her knee was starting to feel better. Her arms were still bright red, and they probably would be for some time to come. She experienced pain in her one wrist but all in all she was improving at a good pace.

All she needed was a cane. If she had one she'd probably be able to hobble around on her own. It wasn't right for Tramp to be here anymore; he was engaged to Ava. Why did her heart squeeze whenever she thought of them together? Probably because she'd have to move. Moving wouldn't be so bad. She could think of it as a new adventure. Sinking back against her pillows she realized she didn't want a new adventure. What she wanted now belonged to another.

She'd have to make a list of suitors, possible suitors. She turned down so many men she wasn't quite sure who was left. It was her own fault; she'd allowed her fears to dictate her life. It was time to grow up and face reality. There would be no bakeshop, there would be no other place to live by herself, and there would be no more independence for her. A tear rolled down her cheek, and she quickly dashed it away. She was strong and now wasn't a time for tears.

Was Judge Gleason still available? He probably thought badly of her now. This whole set up had been doomed to fail from the beginning. Who in their right mind would expect Tramp to take care of her? It must've been some attempt on Shannon's part to play matchmaker.

She wished she could be mad at Shannon but she couldn't. Shannon was really her one and only friend. She'd always been so kind and gracious. Shannon must have thought Tramp would make her a good husband. Shannon should have asked whether or not it was what Ilene and Tramp wanted. She squared he shoulders. *C'est la vie.* She picked up that line while working in the factory in New York City. She'd worked with many French girls and loved the language.

Unfortunately, one of her favorite sayings, this too shall pass, didn't apply to this problem. Marriage wasn't something that passed, having your reputation ruined didn't pass. Her eyes felt dry, and she suddenly realized that her lips were chapped. Carefully, she sat back up and turned her body in order to ease her legs off the bed. She grabbed onto the bedpost and pulled herself up to a standing position. The shaking of her legs gave her pause, but she knew it would stop soon. She clung to the bed post and waited for her legs for steady before letting go. In the past she'd felt lightheaded but not this time. She took a step and her knee protested. Taking another step her ankle wobbled. It probably wasn't the best idea but she wanted some water.

She finally made it to the door jamb and held on for dear life. The water bucket with the ladle was on the kitchen table.

She took a deep breath, willing herself to make it to the table. When she reached it, she sat down, relieved she hadn't fallen. The water made soothing sounds as she swirled the ladle through it then pulled it out. She drank deeply. The cool water slid down her throat until it quenched her thirst. She dipped her finger into the water and then dabbed her lips. There, she felt better than she had in awhile. Maybe tomorrow she could get dressed and sit outside. She'd have to act as though she was well, so Tramp could get on with his life.

She frowned at the thought of Tramp leaving. Of course, she'd see him on the ranch once in awhile but it wouldn't be the same. It was going to be some time before she was able to ride a horse. She stepped as far as she could while still holding on to the doorway and then she stood on her own. The pain was fierce but she'd have to get used to it. A few more steps and she was able to grasp the back of a chair. She put her weight on the chair and eased out a breath.

Without warning, the chair gave beneath her hand and fell backwards sending her flying to the floor.

Ilene stayed there for a moment trying to ascertain if she was hurt more than before. She didn't think she'd done any additional damage, but it hurt like the dickens. Now all she had to do was get up. Sitting, she righted the chair, and with strength she didn't even know she possessed, she pulled herself up until she was able to sit on it. She closed her eyes and slowed her breathing down, gritting her teeth against the pain.

The thunk of the door latch broke the silence, and she pasted a smile on her face as the door was pushed inward. It was important for Tramp to believe she was on the mend and he wasn't needed. The angry expression on his face displaced any of her ideas. Thunderous was what he looked like.

Tramp took long strides until he was next to the chair. He bent and, without uttering a word, picked her up in his arms and put her back into bed. Then he stepped back and shook his head. "What in the name of Sam Houston are you doing?" He stared at her as though waiting for an answer.

"I was just stretching my legs is all." She tried not to wince.

"You aren't in any type of condition to be up and around. What did you need? Water? Or should I go get Shannon for you?"

The worry in his voice made her feel guilty. "No, I just wanted to get out of this room in all."

"You've had your trip for the day. Perhaps tomorrow I can carry you out to the porch for a spell. How does that sound? I'll go get you some water." He didn't wait for a reply, just turned and stalked from the room.

"Wait!"

Tramp poked his head back into the room. "What?"

"What about Gold Dust? Has there been any sign of her?"

"No. I've had people out looking, but so far there's been no sign of her."

Nodding, she lay back against her pillow. "Thanks for trying." Poor horse, she hoped she was able to get her tack off somehow. Though she did have a feeling she'd see her again.

Tramp came in and put the water on the side table. He turned the chair around and straddled it, staring at her as though he had something he wanted to ask her. "Is it men or marriage you're against?"

Startled her jaw dropped. "What do you mean?"

"I mean, do men frighten you, or are you against marriage?"

She narrowed her eyes as she looked him up and down. "Why do you want to know? I can't see how this is any of your business."

"Somehow it became my business. It's up to me to make things right. I can't have people bad mouthing you, now, can I?"

"What in the world are you talking about?"

"You need to get married, and you need to do it fast. Now, tell me, out of all the men in Asherville, which ones do you like?" He folded his arms on top of the chair and gazed at her.

"The only ones I like are already married."

His brows drew together. "What in tarnation is wrong with you? Married men are off limits. You do understand that, don't you?"

A smile tugged at her lips, and she couldn't help but laugh. "What do you think I'm trying to do? I don't want any man and I don't want to get married."

"Well, let's pretend you have to get married. Who would you choose?"

"I'm not playing this game with you. Not now and not ever. If it's the house you're after, I'm almost healed and ready to go."

"That's exactly what I'm talking about. Where will you go? Life is not easy for single females."

What was it going to take for him to change the subject? "Judge Gleason seems like a nice fella."

Tramp's Adam's apple bobbed. "Gleason? Isn't he a bit long in the tooth for you?"

"No, he's a mature man is all. Nothing wrong with that, is there?"

He pressed his lips together. "I can't think of one thing wrong. Judge Gleason it is." Tramp stood up and gave her a curt nod before he left.

Men. They were so contrary. One minute he wanted a name and the next he was not pleased. How could he be displeased with a judge? Did Burt have a deep dark secret she didn't know about? Besides, what difference did it make to

Tramp anyway? He already picked his intended. And Judge Gleason was a safe bet. He'd been a bachelor for far too long to want a wife now.

JUDGE GLEASON? Why him? He hardly even knew how to ride a horse. Well, maybe that was going too far. He knew how to ride, but Tramp would bet he didn't know how to rope. Women didn't flock to him or anything. What was so special about the judge that Ilene would pick him? He sat on the front porch and took a cigarette out of his pocket. He lit it with a match and took a deep draw. No, he couldn't think of one thing that would make the judge a better candidate than him.

Tramp stopped in mid-smoke and ended up coughing. Why did his brain think that? He was not a candidate nor did he want to be one. First thing in the morning he'd find someone to take care of Ilene. Then he'd ride into town and get the judge to come out and spend time with her. The sooner she got hitched the sooner he'd have his house. He was itching to get back out on the range again. So far there'd been no sign of the herd Gold Dust had run off with. He'd find them eventually.

THE NEXT MORNING, Tramp rode into Asherville and tied his horse outside Eats' Place. The restaurant had burned down not too long ago, and it was heartening to see it built again and much nicer than before. Tramp got down off his horse and tied it to the hitching post before he strode in. A few folks nodded in his direction, and he returned the nods of greeting before he made his way to Judge Gleason's table. It was a known fact that the judge did most of his business in two places: Eats' and the saloon. He made it well-known he didn't consort with the women. He just wanted to be where the rest of the men were.

"Good Morning, Judge. Mind if I join you?" Tramp took off his hat.

Judge Gleason wiped his mouth with the cloth napkin and gestured with a sweeping motion of his hand for Tramp to sit down. "Morning. What can I do for you?"

Before he could answer, a young man came rushing toward them. "Howdy, Tramp. Coffee?"

"That would be great, Poor Boy." Tramp grinned. Poor Boy looked more bright-eyed than he'd ever seen him before. He'd been an orphan when Eats took him in. He'd always looked haggard and thin, but now he looked good, not so ill at ease and kind of filled out.

Judge Gleason smiled knowingly. "You haven't seen him for a while, have you? Great changes in that boy. When Eats burned down, Poor Boy went and lived with Sheriff O'Connor and his wife Cecily. He flourished under their nurturing but he loves Eats like a father. When the place was rebuilt, he came back."

"I'm happy for him," Tramp said. He nodded his thanks at Poor Boy when his coffee was served. He took a sip and set the cup down. "The reason I'm here is Ilene."

"She's not worse is she?"

"No, nothing like that. She's lonely, and I remembered you sayin' you wanted to court her. I just thought you'd like to come out to the ranch for a visit." Now that the words were out, Tramp felt foolish. He shook his head. "You know what? Never mind. I shouldn't try to match you two up. It's none of my business." He pushed back his chair.

"Don't leave just yet. You haven't finished your coffee." Judge Gleason stroked his chin a few times then smiled. "You know, I would like to visit with her. I know I was angry with you before, but I know both of you. You're honest people. I believe nothing is going on." He motioned for Poor Boy to come to the table. "Tell Eats the food was great, but I have to get going. You take care."

Poor Boy nodded and hurried away to clear off a table.

"We might as well get going," Judge Gleason said as he wiped his mouth again. He threw down the napkin and stood.

Tramp stood and followed him out the door. They got on their horses and rode off. Tramp was surprised that the judge didn't try to make conversation. He thought really smart people liked to talk, but it was a mostly silent ride. His body became tense with the worry that maybe he was supposed to be the one jawing. He was never so happy to see the house.

Cookie came hurrying out of Tramp's house, and when he saw Judge Gleason he frowned. "Somethin' going on that I don't know about?" His eyes narrowed.

Tramp swung down from his horse. "No. The judge here is visiting Ilene."

"Does she know that?" Cookie's stare didn't waver.

"It's a surprise."

Cookie turned to the judge who was now standing on the ground. "Nice to see you, Gleason." He turned and strode away.

Judge Gleason shrugged and walked toward the house. Tramp quickly followed, hoping he was doing the right thing. Cookie's stare unnerved him, and now he wasn't so sure of his idea to get the judge and Ilene together.

Judge Gleason took off his hat and set it on the table. He ran his hand through his hair and then straightened his jacket. He didn't wait for Tramp, just walked in to Ilene's room unannounced.

Undecided on what to do, Tramp shrugged his shoulders

and walked to the door. He stood just outside, not wanting to intrude, but he was too curious to stay away. Soft murmurs filtered from inside the room. Well, at least she didn't seem upset, yet part of him wondered why she wasn't. She didn't seem like a woman who liked surprises. As much as he wanted to barge in, he had decided on this course of action and he planned to see it through.

He heard the sound of laughter and frowned, taking a step toward the door. Going in would be the right thing to do for propriety's sake of course. Just as he stepped over the threshold he gasped. Judge Gleason had swept up Ilene into his arms. Tramp tried to leave the room without being seen, but it didn't work.

"Oh good," said the judge. "I'll need you to hold open the front door so that me and this young lady can sit on the front porch." Judge Gleason whispered something into Ilene's ear and she giggled again.

None of this sat well with Tramp. He just turned and led the way holding open the door for the couple. Although tempted to sit with them to see what was going on, he decided it best to leave them be. Now that everyone could see Ilene with the judge all pressure was off of him. There'd be no more talk of hasty weddings and wagging tongues. He did however leave the front door open, and he stood by the front window just off to the side so he wouldn't be seen.

After a few minutes, Tramp shook his head in frustration. He still couldn't hear what they were saying. Funny thing, Gleason usually was a bit boisterous and seemed to be used to having people hear what he had to say.

Disappointed, Tramp sat on the settee and waited. This wasn't what he'd had in mind at all. He'd wanted to be free to ride the range, but instead he was too busy keeping an eye on Ilene. He could see her profile from where he sat, and he watched as she nodded eagerly. He hadn't noticed before that she had a dimple on her cheek when she smiled.

Shaking his head, he stood and went to the kitchen and started to pace. Perhaps he never noticed the dimple on her cheek because he never made her smile the way the judge made her smile. His fists clenched and unclenched as he realized what a mistake he'd made by bringing another man into the house.

ILENE'S FACE hurt from smiling at the judge. She tried and tried to concentrate on what he was saying, but her mind kept wandering. Where was Tramp? What did he think about Judge Gleason's visit? Or rather Burt's visit? Somehow in her mind she thought of him as Judge Gleason and not as a Burt. Maybe that was because she didn't like him as much as she had thought she might. He was a nice enough man but he liked to talk about himself an awful lot. He was an important man. Perhaps that's what important men did.

"Don't you think, Ilene?"

Her smile didn't dim as she tried to remember what he'd been talking about. It had to have been something about himself. She wished she could just fake it and say yes but she didn't want to commit herself to something she'd rather not do. "I'm sorry, Judge, er, Burt, I didn't hear what you had to say. The pain in my wrist is worse today than usual, and I can't keep my mind focused. Forgive me?"

Judge Gleason reached over and patted her on her non-injured hand. "Don't you worry none. We'll have plenty of time to talk. I just enjoy spending time with you."

Her constant smile was giving her a headache. Was Tramp coming back? He really shouldn't have left her alone. Was he inside the house?

"And when Tramp suggested I court you, I realized just how much I really wanted to."

Her eyes widened for a brief second and then narrowed. "This was Tramp's idea? Do you think you would've come to the same conclusion if it hadn't been suggested to you by Tramp?" She pretended to be smoothing out her skirt, but what she really wanted to do was hit Tramp. How dare he interfere! Enough was enough. If he wanted his house, he could have his house. "Do you think you could do me a favor?"

Judge Gleason leaned in toward her. "Of course, my dear, what do you need?"

"I know that Keegan and Addie have an unoccupied house on their property since they built the new house for themselves. Do you think perhaps you could ask them if it would be all right for me to come and live there? I'd be more than happy to earn my keep." She watched as the judge drew his brows together and tilted his head.

"Is something going on that I don't know about? Are you in some type of trouble? Is it Tramp? Has he done something to you?" His voice got louder with each question.

"No! It's nothing like that. You see, this house belongs to Tramp, and I'd just feel better if he could have his house back. He's done more than his share to help me, but it's not fair to him."

Judge Gleason leaned back in his chair and relaxed his shoulders. "Sure, I'd be happy to stop over to Keegan's place and see if they'd be amendable to your suggestion. There is, however, another solution. Now, hear me out before you say anything, but you could marry me, my dear. I have a nice house in town, and you wouldn't have to move from place to place ever again. Nor would you ever have to work to earn your keep. I'm not saying I'm any prize, and I've been a bachelor far too long, but I think we could make a go at it. So what do you say?"

He'd startled her, and she was in no way ready to promise herself to a man she hardly knew. She looked up and saw Tramp leaning against the open door staring at her. So he was still here after all. Why? Why had he done this? Was she so hard to get along with or did he simply just not like her? She'd never figure him out and she was too weary to keep trying. So, instead of saying no to Judge Gleason, she found herself telling him she'd think about it.

Both men frowned at her, but she didn't care. If either one of them really had a care for her feelings, they wouldn't have made this whole plan behind her back. It stung her pride that Tramp wanted to be rid of her so badly. It also stung that it hadn't been the judge's idea to come courting.

"I hate to end our little visit, but I'm feeling, oh so tired. I do believe a nice nap would do me good." She didn't look at either man. She wasn't happy with them, and she didn't care which one carried her into her room. She sat stiffly in her chair and she had to keep her jaw from dropping when Tramp stepped forward and swung her up into his arms. It had to be her imagination, but it felt as though Tramp was holding her tighter than usual. Wishful thinking, though. It had to be, for Tramp had no interest in her. Gazing into his glittering eyes, a jolt went through her. He didn't look at all pleased. What had she done now to make him mad?

She hadn't realized how tense her body had become until Tramp set her down on her bed and her muscles began to relax. Gazing past him toward the door, she looked for Judge Gleason expecting him to say goodbye. To her surprise, he wasn't there. Her gaze met Tramp's and held. Why was he so hard to read? He couldn't really be mad could he? After all it was his idea to bring the judge to her. She shook her head. She'd never understand this man.

"Why are you shaking your head at me? What did I do now? Never mind you don't have to answer. Besides, I know you have a lot on your mind. So what will it be? Are you and the judge going to be courting? He's a very respectable man, you know."

"I know he's respectable, and I know he's nice and kind, but I'm going to make my own decisions. Just because you brought him out here doesn't mean I have to marry him. I will of course give it much thought, but I plan to take my time. I know you want your house back, so I've come up with a solution."

Tramp scowled and crossed his arms in front of him. "Is that so? Tell me about the solution."

If only she could she would have walked out of the room and as far away from Tramp as she could get. He treated her as if she was a young girl without a brain in her head. "Burt is going to find out for me whether or not the empty house at Keegan and Addy's place is available to rent. It's really a win for you if it works out. You get your house back and your life back, and you get to have the horses all to yourself. It's what you wanted all along. I can't stay here any longer. I'm not wanted, and I'm not needed. I've become a burden to you, and I apologize. We should have found a different solution instead of having you take care of me. It was really a bad idea."

Tramp ran his fingers through his hair and then rubbed the back of his neck staring at her all the while. "Is that what you think? You think you're a burden, and I want to be free of you?"

Her eyes widened. "Why would I think anything else? You've been kind, and you take good care of me. I appreciate it more than I can say, but bringing Judge Gleason out here tells me everything I need to know. You brought him here to be rid of me."

Tramp shook his head. He opened his mouth as if to speak but said nothing.

"Don't even try to deny it. It's fine really it is. You have your own life to live; you have Ava and a great future together. I want you to be happy, and you can't start your life, your new life, with me here in your way."

Tramp plopped down onto the chair and briefly closed his eyes. When he opened them, a smile spread over his face. "What's this about Ava? We are not together, and I have no plans for a future with her. Where did you hear this little tidbit of news?"

She furrowed her brow. "I got it from the horse's mouth, Ava herself. She told me you plan to get married. Pretty much as soon as I was able to leave. I don't think she has any reason to lie to me."

Tramp chuckled. "So is that what's been on your mind the last few days? I never asked Ava to marry me, though it's true she thought that we were getting married."

Ilene frowned. "You know, Tramp, you're good at speaking in riddles. I never seem to know the truth about where I stand with you. I feel bad that you led Ava on. When she told me about your plans she was serious. It's hurtful when people play with your feelings, Tramp, very hurtful. I hope you talked to her and told her that you don't plan to marry her."

Tramp stood, walked to the window and gazed outside for moment before turning around. "It doesn't sound like you have a very high opinion of me. I'm not one to toy with other people's feelings. Like I said, I never asked Ava to marry me, and I would think that you'd know me well enough by now to realize that. I guess it just goes to show that you don't know me at all. And no I'm not all fired up to get you out of here, so you relax, rest, and heal all in your own time." The whole time he talked he avoided her gaze. He walked out of the room and closed her door behind him.

A sense of loneliness and regret of what could've been cocooned her. No wonder she didn't have any friends; she didn't trust enough for any type of friendship.

CHAPTER SEVEN

*T*hree days later, Ilene was dressed and sitting on the settee in the front room waiting for Shannon and the rest of the quilting bee ladies. She was both nervous and excited. Well, mostly nervous. What if she said the wrong thing? Perhaps they wouldn't like her. Her mouth grew dry, as she began to perspire. She couldn't do it, she just couldn't. She pushed herself up with the aid of crutches Tramp had fashioned for her. She got herself turned around and was just about to head back into the kitchen when Tramp intercepted her before she took so much as a step.

"Going somewhere, darlin'?"

"What does it look like I'm doing?" she snapped at him. When she saw the flicker of surprise in his eyes, she was immediately sorry. "I'm just so nervous. I mean I've met most of the women at one time or another but Tramp, what if I say something stupid or what if I freeze and say nothing at all? I don't know if you've noticed this, but I really don't have friends. I don't know how to make friends."

Tramp gave her a sympathetic smile and gently led her back to the couch. He helped her sit back down then took the crutches and propped them against the edge of the couch. "Darlin' just be yourself. Heck, I like you. Even Cookie likes you, and you know Cookie doesn't like that many people. You're as fine a woman as any of them and don't you forget it. You are just as kind and smart as those women. Sometimes obstacles are put in our path so we can overcome them. Just talk about the latest frou-frous you ladies like."

Ilene sighed. "That's the problem. I don't know anything about frou-frous or child rearing or husbands, for that matter. I just can't seem to find things to talk about."

Tramp's smile made him look very handsome. "How about sharing a recipe or two? I bet they'd love to get their hands on a recipe for one of your pies. Swear them all to secrecy, and it will make them think that you like and trust them. I'm not one for jawing a lot, but I found giving a compliment here and there always helped."

His advice was probably sound, but she still had a knot in her stomach and a lump in her throat. Why was it so easy for some people to make friends and so hard for her? Most of her life she hadn't had to worry about it. She was always with her parents. As far back as she could remember she worked in a factory with her mother. Her mother and father always said it took all three of them working to keep food on the table and a roof over their heads. Too bad her father had spent much of their money on pails of beer. He certainly always had friends around. She tried to give Tramp a smile, but she knew she failed. It was hard for her to put on that plastic fake smile, and she didn't feel she needed to with Tramp.

He gave her shoulder a light squeeze. "Well I have some work I need to get done and Shannon should be here any minute. Keep your chin up you'll be just fine. I have faith in you."

Ilene watched him walk away. A feeling of loss shrouded her.

She shook her head. She was growing to depend on him too much, and that wouldn't end well for her. She'd had enough heartbreak and disappointment in her life. She didn't need more.

But she didn't have long to linger on her negative thoughts before Shannon came through the door.

Though she was always the picture of a wonderful wife and mother, Shannon didn't think so though, not with the long scar on her face. But at least she had stopped trying to hide her face from others. She had on a beautiful lightweight dress made of a pretty fabric of sweet green with the tiniest of flowers.

Ilene took a deep breath and let it out slowly. Shannon didn't make her nervous. It was the thought of the others that made her mouth go dry. "Good morning, Shannon, you look lovely today. I wish I had a way with the needle like you do. You sure do yourself proud with that dress you have on."

Shannon smiled and leaned down giving her a kiss on the cheek. Ilene wasn't sure how to react, so she did nothing.

"You're looking better, Ilene. I'm so glad you're improving. It does my heart good. I have to say I was so worried when Tramp first brought you in, but now you're gaining that healthy glow about you. Cookie should be here in a little bit with the refreshments, and Cinders is spending the morning with our little Olivia."

"Thank you, I do feel better. I'm not up to catching horses yet, but I soon will be. I did want to talk to you about something. I'm thinking about moving off the ranch. Tramp needs his house back, and I have no business being in it. I know Addy has an empty house on her land, and I thought maybe I might ask if I could stay in exchange for working for them."

Shannon sat down at the table across from her and tilted

her head in concern. "Honey, you don't have to go anywhere or do anything you don't want to. There are plenty of people here that need our help. Some of the Plunkett family are still ill."

Before Ilene could answer, Addy and Edith sailed into the house. Addy was all smiles while Edith frowned. Edith looked around as though she was making a mental note of everything inside the house.

Addy set down a big wicker basket on the table. "It's good to see you both. Ilene you look wonderful. I'm glad you're healing. Shannon, you're as lovely as ever. That's a great dress you have on. One of yours?"

"Why thank you, Addy," Shannon said. "It's one of my new ones, and Cinders sent all the way to New York City for the fabric. He surprised me with it."

"He didn't think I had fabric of a good enough quality at the mercantile." Edith shook her head as she eyed Shannon's dress.

A quick knock on the door interrupted the conversation, and Cecily walked into the house. "Well hello ladies. It's so good to see you all. I hope you don't mind, but I invited Ava Plunkett to join us. She should be here in a little bit."

Shannon nodded. "I didn't know you and Ava were acquainted. She's a hard worker and I bet her being with us for a while will distract her from her problems."

Cecily put her basket on the table next to Addy's. "I really don't know her, but she asked if she could join us. I still don't know many people."

Addy and Shannon both laughed. "Well you're getting to know your new husband, Shane. That's bound to take up a woman's time," Shannon said.

Edith tapped her foot. "Ladies, shall we begin? We are here to work, you know."

Ilene watched as Cecily and Addy exchanged knowing

looks. Why was Edith part of the group if they didn't like her? Were they just being kind to her as they were being to Edith?

Cecily sat down next to Ilene. "I heard what happened, and I'm so glad Tramp found you when he did. He seems like a very nice fella. So when are you two getting married?"

Heat swamped Ilene's face, and she was sure she had gone bright red. She didn't know what to say. She hadn't antici-pated having to answer any questions. The longer she was silent, the more piercing Edith's stare became.

"He is very nice indeed," she managed. "And I'm so grateful to him for rescuing me and allowing me to live here. But we're not getting married. As soon as I'm fit, I plan to give him his house back."

"Well, I for one am happy to hear that. You see, Tramp and I are getting married." Ava waltzed into the room and nodded at each of them. "It's very nice to see you all ladies, and I can't tell you what it means to me that you've invited me to join you."

Ilene reluctantly put on her fake smile. She couldn't help but notice how healthy and pretty Ava looked. She had a beautifully curved body that any man would want. Ilene glanced down at her own lean willowy body that was built more for riding horses then for pleasing a man. Funny, she'd never given it all that much thought before, but now the comparison was stark.

Before anyone could say a word, Edith stepped forward and linked arms with Ava. "Well my dear, if you need any help at all planning the wedding you let me know. I'd be more than happy to help you. We haven't had a fun wedding around here in years."

Shannon and Addy and Cecily all exchanged irritated glances. Addy shrugged her shoulders and shook her head.

"So Ilene, did they ever find any trace of your horse? Keegan told me about your amazing way with horses."

"No, Gold Dust never showed up. And I do like working with horses. They seem to take to me. It'll be a while before I'm able to work with horses again, though."

There was a knock at the door, and Ilene didn't bother to get up or ask anyone to answer it. Everyone seemed to just walk in whenever they wanted anyways. Cookie came in and he too had a wicker basket. He winked at Edith as he set his basket down. "Ladies, I have lemonade and cookies here for y'all. Now have fun but don't you dare tire out Miss Ilene." He gave Edith a nod before he left.

"Maybe we should be asking Edith when she and Cookie are going to be married," Ilene remarked. The room fell into silence.

Edith walked away from Ava's side until she stood in front of Ilene, glaring. "That is not your business. I will not be talked about or have any speculation about me. Do you understand?"

She had known it. She'd known she would do something embarrassing. She glanced away from Edith not knowing what else to do. Ilene didn't know the ins and outs of being part of the group but until now she'd always been one to sit back and watch for a while before saying anything. She'd come to think of it as a fault of hers but perhaps it was just being plain smart.

Addy quickly went to her basket and opened it. "Here we are, ladies. I have some of the squares we've been working on. Let's get the chairs set in a circle so we can start sewing. Shannon, have we decided who we are donating this quilt to?"

Shannon quickly helped arrange the chairs in a circle and sat down next to Ilene. "Well, as you know Founder's Day is about two months away, and I was thinking we could raffle off this quilt to help pay the teacher's salary."

Cecily selected a square, grabbed the needle and thread and sat down next to Shannon. "That sounds like a fine idea. The growth of the town is really dependent on a few things, and a school is one of them."

Addy passed out squares to the rest of them before she sat down next to Ilene. "That is a good idea, Shannon."

Edith sat down next to Addy and gestured for Ava to take the last seat. "The town would have to vote on it." Edith settled into her chair still glaring at Ilene.

"Well, I have a suggestion," Ava said. "I'm sure there's plenty of needy families that could use a nice quilt. Since I'm working on this one perhaps someone in my family could use it." Ava smiled and began to thread a needle. "I'm not that much of the sewer, I have to warn you."

The mood in the room seemed to shift, and the attention was no longer on Ilene. It was on Ava, but Ava seemed unaware of it.

"So, Ava, Tramp didn't even tell me that you were getting married," Shannon said as she looked up from her sewing. "You know how men are, but I can't believe you didn't tell me."

Edith smirked. "You didn't know, Shannon? I've known for at least a week now. Tramp must be one of those that plays it close to the vest. I do believe they're waiting for Ilene to be well enough to move on."

Cecily's eyes widened. "Move on? Why Edith that sounds kind of harsh. Ilene, I'm sure she means that they are just waiting for you to get well. You weren't planning on moving on weren't you?"

Ilene felt perspiration form at her brow as her heart beat a bit faster. What was there to say? Tramp had lied to her, and she wanted to cry. "I'm not sure what my plans are. I certainly don't want to stand in the way of Ava and Tramp getting married. I'm just not sure where I'd go. Before the accident I was just given the job by Cinders to work with the horses, but that's going to have to wait for a while. I also made baked goods and sold a lot of them. I just don't know but I think moving on might be the right thing to do. I'll need to find a place to stay while I save up enough to move on though." She ducked her head and pretended to concentrate on her sewing.

She'd counted on Addy to invite her to live on her place but Addy never mentioned it. Surely Judge Gleason had given her the message. She was probably being polite and pretending there'd been no such request.

It was a relief when the conversation turned in the direction of little Ryan and Olivia. It was great fun to hear Addy tell stories of her daughter Peg and her instant dislike of her new brother. Any other time the conversation would have lifted Ilene's spirits, but now all she could think about was how she was standing in Tramp and Ava's way of happiness. She'd thought she had more time to come up with a plan. Shannon wanted her to stay but she didn't think she'd be able to see Tramp and Ava day in and day out. Her heart twisted painfully.

It seemed to take forever for the sewing bee to be over. They had the refreshments, and they did a lot of sewing. Ilene didn't join in any more conversation and she felt odd and very uncomfortable. Finally, Addy stood and announced she needed to get home to Ryan, and Shannon said she too needed to get to Olivia. The women all packed up their things and one by one they left until it was silent again in the cabin. Shannon had even cleared away the refreshments.

It was though no one had ever been there. But they had, and now her hands shook as her heart squeezed painfully. Why had Tramp lied to her? He'd said he wasn't marrying

Ava. It hurt doubly because of the lie. She was so tired of pretending and putting on fake smiles when all she really wanted to do was sob into her pillow. But there wasn't enough privacy for sobs so she'd have to buck up and smile until it killed her.

IT WAS late afternoon when Tramp rode Jack into the yard. He nodded at some of the Plunketts who were sitting outside and headed for the barn. There, he unsaddled Jack, took off his bridal, and let him loose in the corral. "I'll be back in a bit, Jack. I just need to check on something before I brush you down." Tramp closed the gate to the corral and started toward his house. All he wanted was to be sure that Ilene had survived the sewing bee.

Out of the corner of his eye he could see both Ava and Shannon hurrying his way. Something was wrong. He waited for both women to come to him and was surprised at the irritated looks they gave each other. "What's this all about?"

Shannon put her hands on her hips. "I want to know why everyone else knows of your plans to marry Ava and you never told me. I see you every day, more than once a day and you couldn't have told me? Does Cinders know?" She frowned and looked from him to Ava and then back at him again. "I want you to be happy, Tramp, and if Ava makes you happy, then I wish you well. I guess I'm just upset that you didn't tell me."

Ava touched his forearm and smiled up at him. "We didn't want Ilene getting upset, but she's almost better now. Right, Tramp?"

Tramp drew his brows together and blinked. What the heck was going on? "Ava, did you tell people we were getting married?"

"I'm sorry I just couldn't keep it to myself any longer." Her smile fled as Tramp pulled his arm away.

"I'd love to stay and get this all straightened out, but for right now my priority is Ilene." Tramp turned and walked away. Dang it all, why was everything always so difficult? He bet Ilene had to wear one of those fake smiles she hated. It was his fault. He had encouraged her to join the other women. From the sound of it, the day had not gone well.

He walked up the steps slowly and hesitated on the porch for a moment before going in. He wasn't quite sure what to say to her after all he was the one that told her that everything would be fine and she'd make friends. He hadn't counted on Ava being there, but he had thought that the matter was settled. Why did Ava keep up with the charade of them getting married? He sighed and ran his fingers in his hair. He'd have to have a long talk with Ava and make sure this time she truly understood that there would be no marriage.

His heart squeezed when he saw Ilene sitting at the table with her head bowed and her shoulders slumped. This was his fault, and somehow he'd have to make it right. "Ilene?"

She slowly lifted her head and peered over her shoulder at him.

"Hello, Tramp, how was your ride out on the range? Did you come upon any new horses? I keep hoping that Gold Dust would find her way home."

Tramp walked toward Ilene until he was at the table across from her. He pulled out one of the chairs, sat down and reached out to hold her uninjured hand. Was she upset because of Ava or because she thought she had to leave the house? There was so much sadness about her, and all he wanted to do was take her sadness away. He gave her hand a slight squeeze and waited until she met his gaze. "I am not marrying Ava. Why she keeps saying I am I have no idea. I've told her we're not getting married but she keeps persisting. She has Shannon all riled up about the whole thing. In fact, Shannon is hurt that I didn't tell her. I'm not sure what to do. Whatever I say seems cold hearted, but I never asked that woman to marry me."

Ilene stared at him as though she was trying to take his measure and then she nodded. "I believe you. I think there might be something wrong with that girl. But she had us all believing that you two would be wed soon, and I would need to find a new place to live. She made it sound as though I'm standing in the way of your happiness. It was embarrassing to hear it all in front of the other ladies."

Tramp let go of her hand and tucked a stray lock of hair behind her ear. "I wouldn't intentionally hurt you for anything in the world. I'll have a talk with Shannon later, and make sure everything is straightened out, but as far as Ava I'm not sure what to do. I often see her standing or sitting by herself. She's rarely with the rest of the family, and I'm wondering why. I mean she seemed nice enough but she can't go around telling these yarns about me and her. Especially when it ends up hurting someone I care about."

Her eyes softened as she continued to stare at him. "I know Shannon's friendship means a lot to you, and I'm sure you'll get things straightened out with her. I think I'm going to rest for a while." She slowly got up from the table and gave him a smile that wasn't fake, but it wasn't exactly happy either. She grabbed her crutches and hobbled toward her room.

"Ilene?"

She paused and turned.

"I didn't mean Shannon." Their gazes met and held and he could see the questions in her eyes. He didn't say anything more, and she finally broke eye contact and went into her room.

Why did she always seem to think the worst of him? Why couldn't she just admit that they had an attraction between them? He'd seen the way she looked at him at times. He was just beginning to think that maybe they could have something. He'd known all along she didn't want a husband. Somewhere along the line he'd started to think it wasn't a bad idea. Now he wasn't sure what to do anymore. She was so dead set on not having a husband and frankly he didn't think he could change her mind.

The bed creaked when she got in it, and he smiled. He'd go find Shannon and get things straightened out. Enough was enough. Besides, maybe Shannon had a few ideas about how he could keep Ilene from leaving.

ILENE'S HEAD WAS SPINNING. It had been two days since the quilting bee, and things seemed strained between her and Tramp. He spent less time with her, but then again, she was getting better. She hadn't been sure what to make of it until now.

She sat on the settee wishing she could curl up into a small ball and roll away. It seemed Tramp was telling people what they wanted to hear. Pastor Plunkett sat in a chair across from her, looking very apologetic.

"We'll gladly allow you the use of our wagon. We, the missus and I, plan to move into this house as soon as they are wed."

"The use of your wagon? I guess I don't understand." Her heart dropped. Unfortunately, she understood completely. She'd been played for the fool once again.

Pastor Plunkett leaned forward and gave her a nod. "Yes, our wagon. It would be perfect for you, and you'll be right near our other daughters who are also unmarried. I'll be looking to you to chaperone them on any outings. I need them to find husbands."

"Yes, well I'll give it some consideration," she said politely as she fumed.

Pastor Plunkett stood and nodded to her. "It'll all work out. There is a plan for each of us." He walked out the front door and as she watched him from the window she saw his wife hurry to him. They talked with their heads bowed.

It must have been nice to have such faith and to have someone to confide in. The wedding was still going to happen, and she'd done the unthinkable. She'd fallen in love with Tramp. Her heart shattered as she gazed at the wagons outside. Of course she'd be the perfect chaperone. She didn't have responsibilities to keep her home and she wasn't competition for the would be husbands.

All she wanted to do was ride a horse and feel the wind in her face. She'd settle for being able to mix batters and knead dough. Time was wasting away, and she needed to come up with more money. Carefully, she stood and limped into the kitchen, pausing to catch her breath before she continued on to her bedroom. Sitting on the bed, she reached over to the bedside table and opened the drawer. She felt around but didn't feel the old stocking she kept her money in. After telling herself not to panic, she stood and opened the drawer wider. It was gone. Her money was gone!

Ilene slumped down onto the bed. Had she put it elsewhere? She tried to think but in her panic she had a hard time concentrating. When had she seen it last? Tears of frustration filled her eyes. Was it before or after her accident? Taking deep slow breaths, she was able to calm herself enough to logically think things through. She had it before the accident after Cookie had come back from taking her pies to town.

It had to be around somewhere. She leaned over the table

and peered behind it hoping it had been dropped there. Nothing was there. Perhaps under the bed? The thought of getting on the floor almost discouraged her but she didn't have a choice. She needed to find her money.

Slowly she knelt down on the wood floor and then lay so she could see under the bed. Besides a bit of dust, there was nothing. Every muscle in her body screamed at her. She shouldn't have gotten on the floor. How was she supposed to get back up with only one hand in her weakened condition? She sat up and was able to get to her knees and using her elbows on the bed she lifted herself up. Lying in bed had made her weak.

She needed to accomplish two things: getting stronger and finding her money. It made no sense. Who would bother to take what little she had? Her heart dropped. How was she supposed to move out of the house? The pastor's offer was looking better and better. Pressing her lips together, she vowed not to cry. It wouldn't help. Despite her best efforts a lone tear trailed down her face.

If only she could confide in Tramp but he was part of the problem. He kept insisting she could stay. He probably didn't want to hamper her recovery. Whether she wanted to or not, she'd have to talk to Judge— Burt. Ugh, thinking of him as Burt was hard. He'd always be Judge Gleason to her. *Beggars as they say.* She didn't have a choice. Living at Addy's was out. She didn't have a dime to feed herself let alone to set up for baking. It was time to admit the truth and let go. Tramp had been her best friend but not anymore. Not ever again.

She felt steady enough to get to her feet. Slowly she limped outside and headed for the Plunkett wagon. Mrs. Plunkett looked overjoyed to see her.

"My dear, you've made the right decision. You'll be such a help to my girls. I'll have to find out when the wedding will be. I'm sure it'll be soon. I knew you had a good head on your shoulders. Hanging on to a man who is promised to another only leads to heartbreak." Mrs. Plunkett gave her an understanding smile.

"Yes, we need to find out the details. Let me know what you find out," Ilene said. She could hear the quaver in her voice, and it appalled her. She didn't want anyone to know her heart was breaking with every word. She turned, intent on going back to the house when she saw Cookie hitching the team up to the wagon. She might as well go and talk to— Burt and get it over with.

Cookie smiled at her when she approached. "You're looking better every day."

"No, I'm not but thank you for saying so. I have a favor to ask. Could you possibly give me a ride to town? I have some business to take care of." She quickly glanced away, not wanting him to see how upset she was.

"I don't see why not." He paused. "Let me grab a hat out of the barn for you. That sun is scorching today."

Ilene nodded. She hadn't thought to put on a bonnet, and she was too tired to go back for it.

"Here, let me help you up into the wagon and then I'll fetch the hat for you."

It hurt so much getting into the wagon, and she wished she had the choice of staying home but that choice was gone. Her heart beat painfully against her chest. What was she supposed to say to Judge Gleason? What if he wasn't interested in marrying her anymore?

"Here you go." Cookie climbed up, took his seat on the bench, and handed her a hat. "Next stop Asherville, Texas."

He chuckled, and she wished she had as much joy in her heart that Cookie did. Everything inside her screamed at her to go back but she had to be steadfast. The time for choices was over.

CHAPTER EIGHT

ramp peered around the empty house in confusion. Where the heck was Ilene? He'd just come back from the big house so she wasn't there. She must be at the barn. Quickly, he strode to the barn and stepped inside. Rollo was there brushing down a paint named Salty. He looked up at Tramp and nodded.

"Rollo, have you seen Ilene?"

"She's with Cookie." He went back to brushing the horse.

"Where with Cookie?"

"They went to town. You just missed them. Cookie came in to get a hat for Ilene. They'll be back in a few hours, I expect. Is something wrong?"

Tramp shook his head. "No, I was just wondering where she got off to." Shrugging his shoulders he turned and walked back outside. Mrs. Plunkett came hurrying toward him. He was tempted to turn and walk the other way, but it wouldn't be polite.

"I've been hoping to catch up with you, Tramp. You're a hard man to track down." Her smile was so big it almost blinded him.

"I've been around. What's this all about?"

"I like that. A man who doesn't beat around the bush with small talk. I have most things set. I just need a date. Ilene is going to live in our wagon while we live in the house. Ilene offered to chaperone the girls when their beaus start showing up. She is such a dear. So I need the wedding date so I can start packing. I want to take measurements of the windows and such. Curtains need to be made, and that awful settee needs recovering. Don't you worry about a thing. Ava and I will set that house to rights. It needs a woman's touch."

He scowled. "There has been a woman living there. I don't know what touches you're talking about."

"Of course you wouldn't know. Ava has a hope chest filled with table cloths and napkins, doilies, and stitched tapestries to hang. She even has baby clothes all ready to go. Oh, I know it's a bit early to talk of babies but soon. So, you see we have a lot already set up we just need to decide on a date." Her eyes danced with excitement.

He inwardly fumed as he put a rein on his temper. No matter how many times he said he wasn't marrying Ava, everyone still believed they were engaged. How could that be? "Ilene agreed to live in your wagon?" He cocked his right brow.

"Yes, like I said she agreed to it and to be a chaperone."

"Who is going to chaperone her when she goes courting?"

"Tramp, you must realize she's getting to be an old maid, and I don't like to brag, but she'll hardly be seen as a blossoming flower next to my girls. Even she agreed it to be the truth. Facts is facts."

"I see." He didn't see. Ilene was a blossom or whatever Mrs. Plunkett said. Why hadn't Ilene talked to him about it? He'd made his intentions clear. Hadn't he? She must know how he'd come to care for her.

"Tramp?"

"What?"

"I asked about the date. It very important."

"I'll tell you what. Ask Ava what I said when I supposedly proposed. I'm sure we must have set a date."

Mrs. Plunkett's jaw dropped open. "Supposedly proposed? I heard rumors about your character, but I didn't believe them."

"They're probably all true. Good day, Mrs. Plunkett. I have an errand to run." He tipped his hat, turned and stalked to the barn. He quickly saddled Jack and headed toward town.

How on earth could Ilene believe the Plunketts over him? Hadn't he just told her he loved her? He pulled Jack to a stop. Dang! No, he hadn't. He'd never said any pretty words to her. What was she thinking right now? More than likely she hated him. For her to go to town was odd enough. She must have been desperate to get off the ranch.

Nothing was working out the way he had it planned in his head. He had wanted to take it slow, but he'd planned to court Ilene as soon as she was well. "Jack, we need to find that female and quick. Yaw!" They raced over the plains toward town. When they arrived, Tramp swung out of the saddle to the ground. He tied Jack to the hitching post in front of the mercantile. The wagon that Cookie drove was there too.

Taking a deep breath, he entered the mercantile but, to his dismay, she wasn't there. The only people in the place were Cookie and Edith making eyes at each other. It was enough to make him groan. "Howdy. Where's Ilene?"

Cookie pushed off the side of the counter he'd been leaning on. "She wanted to talk to Gleason about something. There's something not quite right with her today."

"Ava's been spreading lies again. I need to talk to Ilene. I'll make sure she gets home." Without waiting for a reply, he was at the door in a few strides and left. More than likely, Judge Gleason was at Eats' Place. Crossing the street Tramp hurried into the restaurant. He scanned the building until he spotted the judge. That was curious. He was alone.

Dodging tables, Tramp made his way over to the judge's table and sat down without waiting for an invite. "Where is she?"

"She left. I offered to escort her, but she doesn't want anything to do with me."

"If you hurt her…" Tramp threatened.

"I think the real culprit is you. I told you that you'd end up tarnishing her reputation. I can't marry her now. That's what she wanted you know. She asked me to marry her. Can you imagine?"

Tramp smiled. "Yes, actually I can." He stood and was out of the restaurant in a flash. He peered up the wooden walkway and down the other side but he didn't see any sign of her. He was about to take a look around when Poor Boy stuck his head out the door.

"She's at the Sheriff's house talking with Cecily."

"I appreciate it, Poor Boy." Tramp gave him a nod of thanks and started walking in the direction of the O'Connor homestead. It was within walking distance from the town.

What would he find? He'd have to worry about that when he got there. No sense inviting trouble. His boot heels clicked against the hard wooden walkway with each step he took. He ran out of wooden planks and walked along the dirt road. It all looked quiet as he climbed the steps to the door. He was just about to knock when the door swung open.

Cecily didn't seem too surprised to see him. "Come on in. Maybe between the two of us, we can figure out what to do."

He took his hat off before he entered the house. "Figure out what?"

"Where Ilene is supposed to go when you get married. I

understand your mother-in-law to be is measuring the place for curtains and the like. Shane thinks that eventually, before you know it, you'll have the whole Plunkett clan in your house."

He rubbed the back of his neck. "Where's Ilene?"

Cecily grabbed her bonnet from a hook near the door. "She's in the kitchen. I'll leave you two alone. Meanwhile I'll try to come up with a solution for Ilene."

He barely heard the door close. He was focused on telling Ilene the truth and making sure she understood it. She probably hated him, and he was innocent. He slowly walked into the kitchen, and what he saw nearly broke his heart. Ilene was sitting at the table with her back toward him. Her shoulders heaved as she cried. Damn, maybe she really did want to marry Gleason. She sounded heartbroken.

He strode until he was close enough to scoop her up into his arms and then he sat down placing her on his lap. He tucked her head under his chin and held against her his chest as he wrapped his arms around her. Rocking her back and forth he tried to give her comfort. She was heartbroken all right, and it was Judge Gleason's fault. Well, he admitted, he had tried to push them together, so maybe he did have a kernel of guilt.

"You're too good for Gleason," he murmured.

She brought her head out from under his chin and stared at him. "The whole town knows?"

"No, of course not."

Her eyes narrowed. "What are you doing in town?"

"I could ask you the same thing. I came to make sure you were all right."

"I never asked for your protection. You were just following me, trying to find out when I'd leave so you can set a wedding date. I do have one option left to me, and I'm going to take it. How hard can it be to chaperone a few girls?"

"I don't know why Mrs. Plunkett asked that of you. You'll end up stealing their beaus."

Her smile was sad. "Thank you for saying that, but we both know I'm an old maid. I never realized how little time a woman had to get married."

"You're not an old maid. I'm sorry you're not marrying Judge Gleason." He wasn't really sorry, but she looked so sad. "I'm not marrying Ava. I told you before how she keeps announcing our engagement."

"That was before her mother came to visit. It's been brought to my attention that I'm selfish staying in your house, when Ava and her parents could be living there." She peered up at him as though searching his eyes for the truth. "I just don't know what's going on. Somehow you and Ava are not of the same mind. She really and truly believes you two are to be married, and her whole family believes it too. I wish I could just say I believe you, but if you had told Ava that you weren't getting married, why she going ahead with making plans for a new life with you?"

She shifted on his lap as though she wanted to get up, but Tramp held her firm. "I have no idea. I've talked to her a couple times and told her we are *not* getting married. I never proposed, but she has it in her mind that we're marrying. Quite frankly, I don't know what to do."

Ilene hung her head and whispered, "I made a fool of myself by proposing to Judge Gleason. I don't know. For some reason, I thought, well actually, I don't know what I thought. I've never felt more mortified in my whole life. He told me my name was sullied. Can you believe that?"

Tramp put his finger under her chin and lifted it slightly until his gaze met hers. "He's a damn fool. I mean, it is a bit unconventional for a woman to ask a man, but he should never have called you sullied. I thought the man had more class than that. You'd think the man would've been flattered. Someday, he'll realize what a mistake he made."

He liked the look of wonder in her eyes as she stared up into his. Perhaps he was making strides after all.

"I seem to be back to where I started," she murmured. "I have nowhere to go, and I can't tell you how awful that feels. When my parents died, I felt the exact same way. It took the three of us working for the small part of the room we called home, and as soon as the money wasn't enough the landlord threatened to put me out on the street. Since then, my life has been utter chaos. I have days when I feel safe and secure and then days like now, where I feel the ground eroding all around me. Cecily said I could stay here for a while, but that's only temporary, and I need a permanent solution. Right now, I think living in the Plunkett's' wagon would be for the best. I'll still be close to the horses, and as soon as I'm 100% better I plan to work with them. I need the money. Somehow mine is all gone." She gave him a slight smile before she pushed herself into a standing position. Then she began to pace. She winced with each step, but she kept going.

"What do you mean your money's gone? Did something happen to it, or did you spend it all?"

"No I was saving so I could maybe open a bakery. I realize I'll never be able to afford to do that now. There are always obstacles in life to overcome, and this is one of them. Cinders will pay me for the work I do with the horses. Eventually, I'll be able to save up enough to go out on my own."

Tramp saw right through her brave front, and his heart squeezed. "Are you in love with Judge Gleason?" His hands balled into fists as he waited for an answer.

Her eyes widened as she shook her head. "No, I'm not. He seems like a stable man, and I thought he was interested in me. I made a big mistake."

Tramp started to relax. It made him smile on the inside that she didn't love Judge Gleason. "I do have an idea about how you can stay in the house."

Ilene stopped pacing and gazed at him. "Oh, really?"

Tramp took a deep breath, feeling like a fool. What if she said no? He squared his shoulders. "If you marry the owner, you'll be able to live in the house forever."

Her jaw dropped, and she turned away from him. The silence lengthened until he wanted to take his offer back. Perspiration formed on his brow, and his heart sank. "Oh heck, I've put you in a bad position. Of course you're not interested in marrying me."

She turned and covered her red cheeks with her hands. "I accept. I'm just sorry it's not a love match. You can take the offer back if you like. It seems spur of the moment."

At least he knew how she felt about him. It wouldn't be honorable to withdraw his proposal, and she'd already had one rejection today. "Of course, I want to marry you. It would solve both our problems. You get to live in the house, and I get Ava off my back. I think it'll be just fine. We get on together, and we have the horses in common, and I can't wait for you to fully heal so I can try your baked goods."

She nodded and gave him a smile that didn't reflect in her eyes. "Yes we do have a good foundation to build on. We haven't worked together with the horses but I think we'll get on just fine. Thank you so much." Her eyes softened. "I really don't know what I would have done without you these last few weeks, and now this."

"I just helped out is all." There was an awkward silence between them. He tried to find something to say but failed. Thankfully, Cecily came through the door.

She smiled at them both. "Ilene you look better. I'm glad."

Ilene nodded.

"You might as well be the first to know. I asked Ilene to be my bride," Tramp said with what he hoped was pride in his voice.

A wide smile spread across Cecily's face. She walked to Ilene and gave her a big hug. "How exciting! I'm so happy for you both. When is the big day?" She took a step back and held on to both of Ilene's hands.

"My goodness we haven't gotten that far yet." Ilene smiled the first real smile he'd seen in a long time.

"There's time enough for the details later. I best get Ilene back to the mercantile so she can catch a ride home with Cookie." Tramp held out his hand and was pleased when Ilene dropped Cecily's hands and took his.

"Congratulations again, and if you need any help let me know," Cecily offered.

Ilene nodded. "Thank you for everything, Cecily. I'm sorry I showed up at your door crying."

"Awe, honey, that's what friends are for." Cecily led them to the front door and opened it for them. "Now shoo, go be happy."

They walked for a few minutes, and when he glanced down at her, Tramp was surprised to see Ilene crying. He stopped and turned her toward him. Her damp eyes tore at his heart. "If you don't want to marry me it's fine. You can still have the house."

She nodded and wiped away her tears. "You are the nicest man I know, and I'd be honored to be your wife."

"Then why are you crying?"

"Cecily called me her friend. It's been a very emotional day. First Mrs. Plunkett and then Judge Gleason making me feel so awful. Now you came to my rescue, and someone besides Shannon called me her friend. It's just so much."

A smile tugged at his lips. "I came to your rescue? I must be one heck of a guy."

"I bet the whole town knows I made a fool of myself asking the judge to marry me."

"Let's not worry about it. Besides, I'm the winner, and Gleason is the foolish one. You ended up with a much better catch." He chuckled as he put his arm around her shoulder. "Let's go, I'm right here beside you."

HIS WORDS COURSED THROUGH HER, leaving her feeling warm inside. Tramp was so different from Judge Gleason. Her face heated, remembering how the judge's eyes opened in surprise and then filled with something akin to disdain. He was polite in his rejection, but it shamed her. The townspeople thought badly of her. She hoped she'd never made any one of the men who had proposed to her feel so low.

Tramp gave her shoulder a slight squeeze, and she gazed up at him, almost tripping. He was doing so much for her. She thought for sure her heart skipped a beat when he smiled at her.

"Don't worry," he said. "You'll be the envy of most of the women once they hear we're engaged." He winked at her.

Her heart lightened at his words, and she laughed. "You think mighty highly of yourself."

"It's just the truth. Come, let's tell Edith the good news. Telling her is like telling everyone. She'll spread the word."

He seemed so sure of himself, and part of her wanted to just sit in the wagon and wait for Cookie. But for Tramp's sake, she'd brave it out. Closing her eyes briefly, she said a quick prayer before entering the mercantile. The bell above the door sounded louder than usual, and she wanted to cringe.

"Good Morning, Tramp. It's nice to see you," Edith said cheerfully before she frowned at Ilene.

Tramp took her hand and led her to a small seating area next to the front window. "It's a great day. Ilene has just consented to becoming my wife." Before Edith had a chance to respond, Tramp sat down on a dainty settee, pulling Ilene down next to him.

Edith's jaw dropped for a moment, and then she frowned. "One proposal a day isn't enough for you?" The bite in her voice sent a chill down Ilene's back.

"She won't have to turn anyone else down. I'm not letting her go," Tramp said lightly.

Edith crossed her arms in front of her and tapped her foot. "I'm not sure I want either of you in my store."

"Of course they're welcome." Everyone turned toward Cookie, who had come out from the back room. "I hear congratulations are in order." He walked over to the couple. He took Ilene by the hand and pulled her up into a big hug. "Happy for you, Ilene." He stepped back and smiled at her. When Tramp stood, Cookie hugged him too. "It's good to know you're home to stay."

There was a bit of moisture in both men's eyes, and Ilene's heart was happy for Tramp. There was a loving bond between the two.

"Humph, Tramp, you can't make her respectable now. Her reputation is too far gone. Then to ask the judge, of all people, to marry her? Who does she think she is going after a man of such high morals and such high standing in the community? It's an outrage."

Tramp stiffened at her side. "I'm not one for gossip, never have been. But I do take exception to you insulting my intended. Come on, Ilene let's go. Cookie, we'll see you at home."

Cookie shot Edith a sharp glance. "Wait you'll need the wagon."

"No, Cookie you stay. Ilene and I can ride double." Without waiting for a reply he whisked Ilene out of there.

As soon as they were on the boardwalk, Ilene pulled her hand out of his. "I can't ride a horse yet."

Tramp touched her arm. "You're shaking. Come on, I'll cradle you in front of me."

She hesitated then nodded. "The sooner I get out of here the better." She walked quickly to Jack and stood beside him waiting for Tramp to mount up first. As soon as he was in the saddle she put her good foot into the stirrup, and with Tramp's help she was soon sitting sideways in front of him. His body was so close to hers, and she felt as though she could draw from his strength.

"Are you comfortable?"

Ilene nodded, and off they went. Not wanting to see censure in anyone else's eyes, she kept her head down until they were out of town. Slowly, she relaxed as they rode. Tramp kept the pace to a slow trot. Cocooned between his arms she felt safer than she had in a very long time. There was bound to be more fireworks when they got back to the ranch. The Plunkett's were going to have fits.

As soon as they reached the edge of the ranch Tramp pulled up the reins and they stopped. "Why are we stopping?" she asked

"I think we need to stretch and rest a bit, plus I want to talk to you."

A feeling of dread spread within as she waited for Tramp to dismount and help her down. It had all been for show. The proposal hadn't been real. Her heart beat painfully against her chest. Once a fool, always a fool. Part of her wanted to just crumble, but a bigger part of her was determined to get on with her life. So, her money was gone and she'd have to live in a wagon for a while. Things could be worse. Couldn't they? No matter how hard she tried she couldn't get the lump in her throat to go away.

Tramp shifted his weight from one foot to the other as he gazed at the horizon. He seemed to be at a loss for words.

"You said you wanted to talk, but you don't have to. I already know what you're going to say." She put up her hand when Tramp opened his mouth. "You've done so much for me and today you tried to save my reputation. But you don't have to marry me. I appreciate all your kindness and your sense of chivalry, but really it's not necessary. I'm going to save enough money to move on. So you see, I do have a plan and you don't have to feel sorry for me or marry me out of pity."

Tramp took off his hat and slapped it against his thigh a couple times. Finally he looked at her. "I already told you, you'd be doing me a favor by marrying me."

"Tramp, you know you can dance out of that situation with Ava. All you need to do is sit down with her, her parents, and Cinders and Shannon. That way there are witnesses when you tell her that you're not going to marry her. So you see, you don't need me. But since you're not going to marry Ava I still have the problem of where to live. Cecily and Shane have an extra room, and I could stay there for a while."

"If you are still hell-bent on saving enough money to move on you have to be at the ranch. Working with the horses is your job, and if you want to get paid you need to do your job. I have enough money saved to lend you what you need to start baking again. This way you'll have your money saved in no time. In the meantime, I'll sleep in the bunkhouse." His brown eyes probed hers, and she wondered what he was really thinking.

"So no wedding?" Her heart squeeze painfully as she

waited for his answer. Why did she care for him so much? He made it clear more than once he didn't want a wife.

"I don't know. The cat's out of the bag, and I don't know how we are going to say the wedding's off when we just told Cookie and Edith we're getting married. I say we should just go along with it. I'll stay in the bunkhouse and you can save your money. We don't have to have a wedding right away, and this way when you leave we can just say we decided it wouldn't work after all." He settled his hat back on his head and held his hand out to her. "We'll have to act happy about our exciting news. Do you think you'll be able to pull it off? I know how you hate fake smiles, so let's just have fun. Deal?"

He was offering her everything she wanted: a place to live, her job working with the horses, and a loan so she could start baking again. Somehow, though, it left her feeling lonely as though she was on her own once again. For his sake, she'd smile and have a good time when they told Cinders and Shannon the great news. He looked so sincere and so handsome, it'd be hard to leave, but she still had time to spend with him. "Yes, let's go and celebrate our independence. After all you've done for me I can put up sitting next to you for the rest of the day. You do realize we'll have to play the part of the couple in love."

Tramp smiled. "I think smiling at each other, me holding your hand and giving you the occasional peck on the cheek will be easy enough. After all we've become good friends. Let's get you back up on the horse and head for home."

As soon as the house was in sight, they could see everyone watching them ride in. Ava's eyes flashed with anger, and her parents joined her, both looking hot under the collar. Shannon was on the porch rocking Olivia. She stood walked down the steps and waited for them to ride in.

"Here we go darlin'." Tramp gave Ilene's waist a slight squeeze. "I do believe this might even be a good time. Don't let the Plunketts intimidate you. After all, you're my intended now, and I'll be at your side." He stopped his horse and got down. He immediately reached up for her and she gasped when instead of putting her down he swung her up into his arms and carried her to Shannon's front porch. He set her down on the bench and took a seat right next to her while drawing her hand into his.

Shannon hurried behind them eyes full of curiosity. "What are you two doing? I've had to spend most of my morning listening to the Plunketts' plans for Tramp and Ava's marriage. And you show up looking like a couple in love?"

Ilene's face heated, and she knew it had turned fiery red. She opened her mouth to explain, but Tramp beat her to the punch.

"Ilene has consented to be my wife." He lifted her hand and kissed the back of it.

Shannon's eyebrows rose. "I'm confused. Ilene, didn't you tell Mrs. Plunkett that she could live in the house and you'd live in the wagon?"

"Yes, I did but that was before I found out that Tramp and Ava were *not* getting married. He never asked her, he never flirted with her, and frankly I have no idea why she would think they were engaged."

Shannon smiled, stood, and handed Olivia to Tramp. She then helped Ilene to stand and gave her a big but gentle hug. "I'm so happy for you, Ilene, so very happy. Tramp is really getting a prize. Best of all you'll be able to stay right here on the ranch. I was worried that you'd leave, and I'd be so lonely without you." She stepped away from Ilene and bent down to give Tramp a kiss on his cheek. "Congratulations!" She took Olivia from him and sat down in a rocking chair.

Tramp stood and put his arm around Ilene's waist. "I'm one lucky cowboy." He turned and kissed her cheek.

Ilene couldn't help but stiffen at Tramp's kiss. It made her heart flutter, and that she couldn't allow. Out of the corner of her eye she saw Ava and her parents all marching in their direction with great big frowns on their faces.

Mrs. Plunkett arrived first with her hand over her heart. "My word is this any way for an engaged man to act? Ilene, kindly step away from him. This is just unseemly." She shook her head and directed her gaze to Tramp. "I finished measuring windows for new curtains, and I have a list of other improvements I plan to make." Then she stared pointedly at Ilene until Ilene's knees went weak and she sat down. When Tramp sat next to Ilene the look of fury on Mrs. Plunkett's face was downright scary.

"Tramp, would you mind explaining yourself?" The pastor asked. He crossed his arms and tilted his head, waiting for an answer.

Ava climbed the steps, gave Tramp the evil eye, and then she proceeded to push Ilene off the bench.

Ilene landed with a thump and lay still for a moment trying to figure out if any part of her was reinjured. She started to get up but Tramp was by her side in an instant. He knelt down next to her and cupped her cheek with his hand. It was such a sweet gesture, and she wished with all her heart that it was real.

"Ilene, are you hurt?" He didn't wait for an answer, just helped her up and seated her back on the bench. He turned and shook his head at Ava. "What is wrong with you? Ilene has done nothing to you, and it's unconscionable that you would push her. She's still healing from her fall from the horse."

Ava put her hands on her hips and took a step forward toward Tramp. "You're my man, and she shouldn't be enticing you. I see the way she looks at you. She wants you for her own, and if you can't see that, then you're a fool. I'm sure Shannon will see to it that Ilene gets home. I think you should spend your time with me."

Ilene briefly closed her eyes. Was it so obvious how she felt about Tramp? Ava said she could see it, and maybe everyone else did too. Her heart hurt. This engagement was not a good idea. There was no way she was going to be able to walk away unscathed.

"Ava you know I never asked you to marry me. Not once did I even suggest such a thing. I haven't courted you I haven't toyed with your emotions or otherwise. You keep telling people we're getting married but that's not the truth, and you know it. It's time to put all this nonsense to an end once and for all. In fact, I have asked Ilene to be my wife, and she did me the honor of consenting." He folded his arms in front of him and stared at each of the Plunketts, one at a time, as if he was daring them to deny what he said.

Pastor Plunkett stepped forward. "Of course, you've toyed with her emotions. Why would she tell us not once but twice you proposed? It makes no sense. Ilene seemed to know. She was willing to move into our wagon after you and Ava were wed. I'm afraid I'm going to have to insist that you keep your promise of marriage to my daughter." His voice grew louder with each word until everyone within the area all turned in their direction.

Tramp lowered his hat and widened his stance. He looked like a man who'd had enough and was trying to rein in his temper. "Out here in the West, a man's word is his bond. Calling a man a liar is about the worst thing you can call him. I'm sure you didn't mean to insult me by insinuating that I proposed to Ava. I told her we're not getting married. I told her I never asked her to be my wife. I think, as her parents, you need to have a long talk with her about what being truthful means. I refuse to allow her to drag my name through mud due to a lie. Now, if you'll excuse us, we were celebrating our good news here with Shannon and we'd like to get back to it." Tramp stepped forward until all the Plunketts had left the porch and gone back to their wagons.

He sat down on the bench next to Ilene and took her hand in his. "That girl is plain loco, and the fact that her parents believe her makes my stomach turn. I'm hoping this is the end of it." He gave Ilene's hand a quick squeeze as he smiled at Shannon. "This is supposed be a happy day, and I'm sure sorry that Ava tried to ruin it."

"Ava can't take away the happiness that's in your heart. Anyone who looks at the two of you can see how much you love each other. I saw it a while ago, and it amused me to no end that neither of you seemed to know how the other felt." Shannon stroked Olivia's back when she started to fuss. "Before long, you'll have one of these too. Just imagine your children and mine will grow up together."

Ilene's eyes widened and her breath hitched in her chest. She hadn't thought that far ahead. Of course, there wouldn't be any children since it wasn't going to be a conventional marriage if they ended up getting married at all. She didn't want to lie to Shannon, so she just smiled and nodded. Tramp moved his leg until it touched hers. A warm shiver floated through her body at his touch. She was tempted to move away, but she didn't want it to look odd, so she sat there holding hands with Tramp while their legs touched.

"Shannon, I meant to ask you," Ilene said. "Do you know if anyone has been in my bedroom? I know I was asleep a lot so I just assumed that it was just you, the doctor, and Tramp who had been there."

Shannon shook her head. "Why do you ask? Did something happen?"

Ilene sighed. "It appears that my money has gone missing. I hid it in the sock and put it into the drawer of the table next to my bed. I looked and I can't seem to find it. It was all the money I'd made from my baking." Her shoulders slumped.

"Perhaps you moved it and forgot? Tell you what, I'll come by tomorrow, and we'll search for it. I'd suggest that Tramp help you, but now that you're engaged it wouldn't be proper for him to be in your bedroom. Kind of funny if you think of it. He stayed there and helped you, and it was perfectly fine, but now that you're getting married the rules have changed."

"I should probably tell you about how I made a fool of myself in town today. It's bound to get back to you anyway." Ilene paused it took a deep breath before continuing on. "I asked Judge Gleason to marry me. He said no, but it was the way he said it that upset me. It wasn't a gentle let down. His eyes actually widened in horror as though I was suggesting something too terrible to think of. He told me that he couldn't possibly marry someone with such a tainted reputation. I ended up fleeing Eats' in tears."

Shannon gave her a reassuring smile. "I know what it's like to have the townspeople talk about you. But I've learned that the ones that talk about you would never have been your friend anyway, so really you're not missing out on much. I know it can be hurtful, and I don't go into town very often, but really, try not to worry about it."

"I wish I could just brush it from my mind. But you're right, if people want to talk about things that aren't true then we would never have been friends in the first place. Funny, my mother would've given me the same advice."

"So tell me, did you set a date yet?"

Ilene opened her mouth to answer, but Tramp beat her. "We've decided to take it slow. I want to be sure that Ilene is all healed up first. Plus we have some mustangs to catch. I'm going to stay in the bunkhouse, and Ilene will have the house."

Shannon nodded. "Well that gives us time to plan a real nice wedding. This is so exciting. My own wedding was a hurried affair with Judge Gleason presiding."

Ilene's heart jumped into her throat. She couldn't keep lying to Shannon.

"Well, Ilene, what do you say? We should probably get back to the house so I can pack my things. Plus we do have a lot to talk about don't we sweetheart?"

As soon as Ilene stood Tramp took her hand in his. He was going to drive her crazy with all this touching. "Thanks for being happy for us, Shannon, it's been a difficult day for Ilene but I think it's ending on a better note then it started."

"Yes it has. Thank you, Shannon. I'll talk to you in a bit. I think I'm well enough to start helping with supper again."

"Ilene, don't you dare show your face over here. You only get engaged once. I'll send Cookie over with supper for both of you. Now shoo I need to put this little one down."

Tramp nodded and tipped his hat to Shannon. "That's mighty nice of you. Tell Cinders I'll talk to him later."

Ilene's emotions were high as she walked hand-in-hand with Tramp to his house. Part of her was tingling from his nearness, but she was troubled about deceiving her best friend. The smiling part and pretending to be happy wasn't very hard at all and she wished these were real moments of happiness.

SOMEHOW, there was a certain rightness of having Ilene's hand in his. He'd always thought her attractive, but lately she'd been downright beautiful. He was just as upset as she was that someone had taken her money. But it was keeping her on the ranch longer. Marriage to her would not be a hardship, but that wasn't what she wanted. Perhaps he could try to change her mind, but he had no intention of playing the fool.

He had plenty of time to get it all figured out. They walked into the house and suddenly he felt awkward. He didn't know what to say. He certainly didn't want to talk about how if they waited long enough they wouldn't have to get married.

"You can use that crate over there in the corner to pack your things in."

He grinned at her. "Can't wait to be rid of me?" He watched as she turned a beautiful shade of red.

"It's not that." She ducked her head so he couldn't see her eyes. "I just want the gossip to die down. I was wondering one thing though. Would you expect your wife to stay home every day or would she be allowed to ride the range chasing mustangs?"

"Now this wouldn't be one of those trick female questions would it?"

Her gaze met his, and she smiled. "Why, whatever do you mean?"

"You know, for instance, say you bought a hat that was just plain ugly. You'd asked me if it looks nice on you. Now I'd be in a pickle. If I tell you the truth and say it's ugly, I risk your wrath. So I just smile and tell you what you want to hear."

"This isn't the same at all unless the truth is you really would expect your wife to stay home. Never mind, you don't need to answer the question I know the answer." She turned from him and added water to the coffee pot.

What had just happened? They had been all smiles and minute ago. Women certainly were complicated creatures. "That's not what my answer is. We are going to ride and catch mustangs together. If we end up marrying, we'll still ride and catch mustangs together. When you care about a person, her happiness becomes important to you."

She turned around and stared into his eyes. "You know for the amount of time we've spent together I really don't know much about you. And for the record I like your answer. But...I don't know your favorite color or your favorite meal. I don't know many of your likes or dislikes."

"My favorite color is blue, and nothing beats a nice juicy steak. I don't like being pushed into a corner, but I do like you. I also like horses and cattle. Long days in a saddle don't bother me, and I believe that you have to work for what you want. I also believe in second chances and someday I want a family of my own, including children."

She stared at him as though she was contemplating his words. He thought for sure he'd get some reaction from her when he mentioned children, but she just seemed to take it all in as matter-of-fact.

"Your turn to tell me things you like and don't like." He pulled out a kitchen chair, turned it around and straddled it as he sat down.

"I like the color yellow, and I'm not sure what food is my favorite. I'm just grateful when I have food. I like to bake, and I'm good at it. I seem to have a way with horses, even though I'd never touched one before coming here. I love the feel of the wind on my face and my hair whipping in the wind behind me as I ride. I'm shy, and I have a horrible time knowing what to say. And I too would like to have children someday. You know, even though I made a fool of myself with Judge Gleason, I'm kind of proud of myself."

"Proud?" he asked as he tilted his head.

"It took everything I had to walk into Eats' and up to the judge. The fact that I even got any words out it all is amazing. There'd been so many times in my life that I wanted to do something but I didn't because of my shyness and my fear of what others might think. So yes, I'm proud that I was able to do that even though it turned out to be a disaster."

"You fascinate me. You really do. And I have to admit I'm proud of you too. It's not easy to conquer fear not easy at all. You did good. If you think about it we got a lot accomplished today. You never need to be shy around me, remember that." He stood, began to collect his things and put them in the crate. "Are you sure you'll be alright alone?"

"I can manage thanks to you. Besides, it's time you got back to your horses. I think I'll be able to join you in about a week. It'll sure be nice to ride a horse again."

Tramp grabbed his crate and started to walk toward the front door. "What do you think you're doing? You can't leave now. Shannon thinks we're celebrating, and if you leave so soon it'll look suspicious."

Tramp sighed and nodded. "You're right. How about a game of poker?"

Her smile lit up her face. "Now poker is a game I'm good at. My father taught me."

A grin tugged his lips upward. "Good, that should make it interesting. We'll play for a couple hours in front of the window so everyone can see we're spending time together in a wholesome way."

CHAPTER NINE

*I*lene stood peering out the front window watching the Plunketts gather the last of their things. Pastor and Mrs. Plunkett both insisted that Tramp do the right thing by Ava. It was scary for a few moments when Pastor Plunkett drew his gun and aimed it at Tramp. Luckily, Cinders had stood behind the pastor and was able to grab the gun without anyone getting hurt. It was then decided it would be best if the Plunketts went their own way.

Sighing, Ilene had to admit it was a relief to have them leave. Every time she left the house the whole Plunkett family stared at her with anger and disdain. It had been nerve racking, and she felt herself withdrawing little by little.

Tramp came to visit every day, and they always sat outside on the front porch in full view of everyone. Ilene had hoped that they'd be able to get to know one another even more, but it was hard to carry on a conversation while they are being stared at. They never mentioned getting married, their hopes and dreams for the future, or setting a date.

It was what she had signed up for, so she really couldn't be mad at Tramp but the disappointment of not getting married ate at her. Soon enough she supposed people would start asking questions, but for now it felt as though her life was in limbo.

She never did find her money. Both she and Shannon had looked high and low throughout the house but they never found it. Shannon offered to lend her money, but she refused. Her life was too unpredictable at the moment.

She watched as Cinders and Shannon bid the Plunketts farewell. She didn't dare go out there, she wasn't welcome. She stared out the window hoping to catch a glimpse of Tramp but he was nowhere to be found. Now that he didn't need to keep Ava at bay, she wondered if he'd come to visit her today. Probably not. Shrugging, she turned away from the window and walked to the kitchen.

The shirt she was making for Tramp lay on the table. She'd been so excited when she started it, knowing that he'd love it, but now she wasn't sure he'd appreciate it. Would he announce the fact that they'd broken their engagement today or would he wait? Her heart squeezed. Sitting down at the table, she decided she might as well finish the shirt. She picked up the needle and thread and began to sew the pieces together.

The house was so empty and terribly quiet. While she always longed to live by herself she now felt so very alone. She was still in the same situation she'd been in, nothing had changed. She needed to find a place to live and it weighed on her mind.

Tomorrow, tomorrow would be the day she'd start riding again. She often wondered what had happened to her horse Gold Dust. She just hoped she was safe and happy. Maybe she'd see her again in her travels. Yes, it was time to get her pants out and get back to work. Part of her was thrilled to be working with Tramp, and another part of her didn't want to spend her time with him. It hurt too much to know he didn't care for her the same way she cared for him.

THE NEXT DAY, Ilene got up early, dressed in her pants and long shirt and hurried to the barn. She got many welcoming neighs from the horses, and that lifted her spirits. She grabbed the bridle and opened Chuck's stall. She easily put the bridle on his head and led him out into the middle of the barn so she could saddle him. The saddle was much heavier than she remembered. Apparently, she hadn't gained all her strength back.

Soon, she had Chuck ready to go. She grabbed the cowboy hat that she sometimes borrowed and they left the barn. The sun was barely coming up, and all was quiet. Soon enough, the place would be filled with all the hands wanting breakfast and lots of coffee. It took two tries, but she mounted up and off they went.

As soon as the house was out of sight, she whipped off her hat and let her hair fall around her shoulders and down her back. This is what she missed, this feeling of freedom, the feeling that she could do anything she set her mind to. "Come on, Chuck, let's go for a run."

Chuck was willing and eager to run, and it felt glorious. The sunrise was so beautiful, all fiery orange and yellow, and the smell of the grass and flowers all rose to greet her. Never in her wildest dreams while she was growing up in New York did she ever think she'd be on a horse. She smiled. Even if Tramp didn't want her, she would find some way to stay. This was now her home.

She slowed Chuck down to a walk as they got close to the pond she liked to swim in. She heard a horse call and Chuck whinnied a response. She scanned the area but didn't see another horse. Cautiously, she went in the direction of the horse's call. They were close to the pond now and in the dense foliage of the trees when she spotted her horse. She quickly got off Chuck and ran to Gold Dust.

Tears flowed down her cheeks at just how thin she had become. Her bridle had become entangled in tree branches and her face and neck were full of blood. The saddle was gone as were the reins but the dang bridle held the mare prisoner. As soon as Gold Dust caught wind of her scent, she glanced in her direction. Her eyes grew wide as she tried to struggle to break free from her bonds. Gold Dust didn't seem to recognize her at all.

Slowly she walked to the horse but made sure she was out of kicking distance. "Gold Dust, it's me. I won't harm you. Oh, my poor baby, how long have you been stuck here?" She took slow, small steps toward her talking to her softly, trying to calm her. One of her hooves looked to be at an odd angle and Ilene feared the worst.

Gold Dust stood still as Ilene detangled her and took the bridle off. The mare could walk, but she limped badly. She headed toward the pond and began to drink. Ilene's heart sank. She could see her horse's ribs and hip bones. The horse obviously hadn't been getting enough to eat these last few weeks. As soon as she had her full of water she raised her head and looked at her. Gold Dust neighed in greeting and took a step in Ilene's direction.

Gladness filled her when the mare recognized her, and she gave her a big smile as she edged closer to her. She patted her neck and tried to soothe her. Gold Dust had several cuts all over her body. "My poor baby, what happened to you?" The horse would make it home, she just knew it, and she took a deep breath. Gold Dust would have to make it back home, she'd never had to put a horse down before.

She walked to where Chuck stood outside of the trees,

surprised that Gold Dust followed her. She walked to her and stroked her as she took full measure of her injuries. She cried a bit more before she grabbed her shotgun. It was going to take every ounce of inner strength to shoot her friend.

Just as she decided to end the suffering, she caught a glimpse of a cowboy riding pell-mell toward her. It was Tramp, and hope sprang in her heart. At least she wouldn't have to do this alone. She continued to talk to Gold Dust as she waited for Tramp to reach them. She couldn't stop the tears from flowing but she didn't care.

"I see you found Gold Dust." He swung down off his horse and slowly walked to where they stood. "It looks like you've had better days," he murmured to the horse.

"I was just about to put her down. I'm glad you're here with me."

Tramp took her hand and gave it a slight squeeze before letting it go. He walked around Gold Dust examining the mare's cuts, and finally he squatted down and ran his hands along the horse's injured leg. "Let me see her walk."

Ilene nodded and took a few steps while Gold Dust followed. Tramp sighed loudly.

"I know what needs to be done and I'm ready to do it." Her heart squeezed, she'd never killed before.

Tramp took the rifle from her hand and placed it on the ground before he drew her into the circle of his strong arms. He stroked her back, and she calmed at his touch, allowing herself the luxury of being with him for only a moment. She needed to get this done and over with.

"I don't think she needs to be put down, murmured Tramp."

She took a step back and gazed into his eyes, wondering if she had heard him correctly. "What are you saying exactly?"

Tramp gave her one of his killer smiles. "Her leg isn't

broken. It looks more like a bowed tendon to me. It'll take a few days to get her back home, but I think between the two of us we can do it."

She tilted her head and stared at Tramp. "She can be saved? We can't leave her out here by herself."

"This is what I think we should do. We walk her the bare minimum toward home each day. Me and some of the boys can sleep under the stars each night. I mean we really aren't that far from the barn, but far enough that we have to take it very slowly with Gold Dust."

Ilene nodded. "I like your idea except for the one part. I plan to sleep out here with my horse." Tramp opened his mouth and she put her hand up to stop him. "Don't try to talk me out of it. Don't tell me I'm wrong. And I couldn't care less what everyone else thinks. I'm certain this will be the talk of the town, and I'll be considered scandalous once more but that's too bad. My horse comes first."

Tramp took her into his arms again. "You realize that if we do this, we'll have to get married for sure. There'd be no walking away from each other, no changing our minds, and I want the marriage to be a real one."

"Of course it'd be real. I've never heard of a fake marriage."

Tramp slowly let her go and walked over to his horse Jack. He reached into the saddlebags and drew out some oats. Taking off his hat he threw the oats into it and then he put it in front of Gold Dust. "Now I'm just going to give you a little at a time. I'm not sure how you ended up so skinny, but I don't want to overload your belly. Small and frequent feedings will be the way of things for a while." He stood there in front of Gold Dust, holding out his hat until Gold Dust ate every last oat. "I'm not sure you understand what I mean by a real marriage. There can be different kinds of marriage. For example a marriage of convenience."

Ilene shook her head as she stared at Tramp. "I'm not sure I know what that means."

Tramp slapped his hat against his thigh before adding a bit of water to his hat for Gold Dust to drink. "I guess what I'm trying to say is I want you in my bed. I want to have the usual relationship a husband and wife have."

Her face heated as she looked at the ground. She'd been trying to avoid this very thing, but now she really didn't have a choice if she wanted to save Gold Dust. She'd have to join with the rest of the women in their pain. She'd end up just like her mother crying and pleading every night. Or perhaps she'd be the type of woman that woke up every morning with fresh bruises on her. She lifted her head and stared at Gold Dust. She could do this, she could be a good wife if she had to.

"Would being married to me be so bad? I mean we're already friends, and we get on just fine. Besides I like having you in my arms."

She felt his eyes on her. He was waiting for an answer, and part of her just wanted to run. She was downright scared. "Yes I mean no. I mean yes I'll marry you." She glanced at him quickly and was surprised at the look on his face. He seemed happy about this marriage thing.

The next thing she knew she was in Tramp's arms and he was swooping down to kiss her. Her body tensed and she put her hands between them fully intending to push him back. His strong lips on hers ceased all thought. She'd never felt anything so intense before. She'd never felt so close to anyone before. She opened her mouth to him and he caressed her tongue with his.

Her heart felt so full of wonder, hope, and love, it shook her to her core. She managed to get her hands out from between them, and she put them around his neck before she knew it, she was pulling his head down for more kisses. She opened her eyes as they kissed, wanting to see what he looked like, fully expecting him to have his eyes closed. But they weren't. He was watching her too. She wondered at the look in his eyes. He looked happy, but that didn't mean he loved her.

He stopped kissing her and caressed her cheek with his calloused hand. Staring into her eyes, he smiled. "I'm looking forward to being your husband."

Tiny chills went through her body at his words. Part of her wanted more than kissing but a bigger part of her was afraid. She had no words to express how she felt so she simply nodded and hoped she was doing the right thing.

"I'll head back to the house and grab enough stuff for us for a few days. I'll let Shannon and Cinders know what's going on. Is there something I could bring for you?"

"A change of clothes would be nice. I'm so relieved we plan to save Gold Dust. If you hadn't have come when you did I would have put her down." The thought of what she had almost done made her shiver.

"We still might have to put her down, but this way we are giving her a fighting chance. I'll be back in a couple hours. In the meantime, let Goldust rest. I'll get something to put on her leg." He pulled her close again and gave her another kiss before he left.

TRAMP DREADED the questions he'd get from Shannon when he told her his plan. Even he wasn't sure if it was a good plan. Somehow, he had ended up proposing to Ilene for real. Shaking his head, he wondered what had gotten into him, insisting on making their marriage real. That had not been his plan at all. The original plan of her leaving and breaking off the engagement was the plan he wanted. Wasn't it? Oh heck thinking after kissing was never a good idea. He rode to the barn and jumped down off Jack's back.

"Rollo, would you mind feeding and watering Jack here? We'll be riding back out in a little bit."

Rollo nodded. "Sure thing, boss." He grabbed the reins and led Jack into the barn.

Tramp headed toward Shannon and Cinders' house. Shannon was sitting in the rocking chair rocking Olivia just as she did every day.

"Hello, Tramp, beautiful day isn't it?" Motherhood suited her. She was more lovely than ever.

"Hello to you too. Ilene found Gold Dust, and she's been hurt. I mean to bring the horse home slowly. Might take a couple days. I'm gonna need some supplies for me and Ilene."

Shannon's eyes widened. "What exactly do you mean by you and Ilene?"

Tramp shrugged. "You know Ilene, she's very headstrong. I told her that me and the boys could handle it, but she wants to be with Gold Dust. I figure since we're getting married anyways, it doesn't make much difference if she stays out there with me."

Shannon bit her lip and appeared lost in thought. "She's a grown woman, and she's made her choice. She chose you, and that's fine by me. Cinders and I will bring the pastor out to you after church tomorrow. He loves Cookie's cooking so I'm sure he won't mind."

Tramp leaned down and gave Shannon a quick peck on the cheek. He stood and smiled. "That sounds great thank you, Shannon. I need to get the supplies I don't want to leave Ilene out there by herself for too long. You know for such a shy gal, Ilene has a stubborn streak in her. Did I ever tell you the first time I met her she pulled a shotgun on me?"

Shannon laughed. "She's got a lot of grit and gumption. She's braver than she knows. Sometimes she's just a bit unsure of herself, but if anyone can help her get over that it would be you. Now, get the things you need to go. You don't want to leave her out there by herself too long."

"I'm gettin'. I'll see you tomorrow. Just head toward the old pond and you're bound to see us." He went into the house and grabbed some salve for Gold Dust. Cookie always made the best salve. Next, he grabbed some food and put it all in a burlap bag.

Shannon hurried to her bedroom and came out with a burlap wrapped package. "I made this for Ilene. It's a dress. I saw how you both looked at each other and decided she needed a wedding dress."

He took the package from her. "I know she'll appreciate it." He nodded to Shannon as he went back out the front door and made his way to his house.

His house. That was the way he thought of it all along. Soon enough he'd think of it as his and Ilene's house. His heart turned over, remembering the kiss he had shared with Ilene. She was one heck of a gal. He grabbed some clothes for the both of them and a few supplies before he hurried back out the door and rushed to the barn.

After thanking Rollo, he re-saddled Jack. Soon he was on his way back to his lovely bride to be. Their marriage should be a good thing. He'd sensed a bit of reluctance on her part, but she'd get over it. Did she even know what a wedding night entailed? Tomorrow, she'd be his wife and he couldn't get the smile off his face as he rode.

It wasn't a far ride to where he'd left them. Ilene stood under the canopy of trees and talked to Gold Dust as she stroked her nose. It would have been a perfect sight if Gold Dust wasn't in such bad shape. They'd get the weight back on her with care and time, but who knew how much the horse had suffered in the last few weeks?

If anyone could sweet talk a horse, Ilene probably could.

He'd never seen her in action, but he'd be interested in watching her do just about anything. When he'd started to feel this way about her he wasn't sure.

"Howdy. Shannon says hello." He jumped down off Jack and gathered the items he'd brought. The first thing he got out was the salve for Gold Dust's leg. He patted the distressed horse on her side and went to bend over to lift her leg. Without warning, the horse kicked out. Tramp jumped back in the nick of time.

"Whoa, Gold Dust," Ilene said. "Do you have a rope?"

I'll get it," Tramp said as he watched Gold Dust settle down. He went back to Jack and removed the rope he had hanging from the saddle. As he walked back to Ilene, he said softly, "I'll put it around her neck."

"No, just give it to me."

He wasn't happy about it, but he handed her the rope. "You could get hurt you know."

"I know." She looped the rope around the horse's injured leg and gently lifted it. Gold Dust stood perfectly still. "Hand me the salve will you?"

Tramp handed it to her. "I thought you'd never really been around horses before."

"I haven't. It's fine Gold Dust. This will help you walk better. Yes, girl." She rubbed some of the salve on the leg.

Tramp was ready to grab Ilene out of the way if the horse became unwieldy. To his surprise, Gold Dust turned her head and looked at Ilene, and then looked straight ahead again. Tramp had never seen anything like it.

Ilene stood and released the rope. "There. The first of many hurdles, I expect."

"I brought another bridle but I don't think she'll allow it."

"Probably not. Her face is so cut up. For now we'll just let her be. I doubt she'll wander far. We can try to get the rope around her neck tonight but I'm not sure. We'll wait and see."

Tramp nodded, keeping his eyes on Ilene's face which was so full of excitement. He smiled. "You light up when you talk about horses."

"I've been blessed. I've received many gifts from God. I have skills for baking, and now I have skills to help horses. It fills me with joy. I just hope I have the skills necessary to make a good wife."

"Oh, about that. We're getting hitched tomorrow. Shannon is bringing the pastor here after church."

Her body stiffened and her smile drooped. "Tomorrow?"

"Ilene, tell me what's wrong. What is the real reason you turned down every proposal?" He tried to make his voice as gentle as possible.

She turned her back on him and walked a few steps away. "I'm afraid. You see, growing up in the tenements of New York, the walls were thin. Most families couldn't afford their own rooms so we were squeezed together without room for privacy." She paused for a bit. "The married couples weren't discreet or quiet. What I heard from most women were terrifying screams. There were pleas for the men to stop. I'm afraid. I know all married women go through it, but I'm not sure if I can. I'll only disappoint you."

Tramp walked over to stand behind her and wrapped his arms around her waist. "It isn't always like that. If a man cares and takes his time, it can be very pleasant."

"Pleasant?" She turned in his arms and gazed up into his eyes as though she was searching for the truth.

"Yes, my sweet, pleasant. There are some women who enjoy it."

"I don't see how—"

He bent his head and touched his lips to hers very lightly. He gave her a few gentle kisses before she wrapped her arms around him and brought his head down for a proper kiss.

This time it was she who deepened the kiss and his heart began to thump.

"My knees feel weak, Tramp." The questions in her eyes delighted him.

"That means we're meant to be together."

"Did anyone else's kiss make you feel that way?" she asked.

"Not like yours, never like yours."

She nodded as she broke from the circle of his arms. She appeared to be confused and uncomfortable. "I guess we should gather wood for a fire," she suggested.

Feeling her need to be alone, Tramp nodded. "I brought some soap. I figure we can take turns bathing in the pond. I want to look my best for the wedding."

"Me too, thank you."

LATER THAT EVENING, Ilene placed her bedroll near the fire. She was too keyed up to sleep. Perhaps she should have gone back to the ranch to sleep. She could imagine the scowl on Edith's face when she heard. Tramp had brought her a nightgown to wear but she didn't feel brave enough to change into it. It was nerve-racking enough bathing in hearing distance from him. Of course he was the perfect gentleman but she couldn't get rid of the panicky feeling inside of her the whole while.

She took Tramp's bedroll and placed it on the other side of the fire but further back from its warmth. She glanced at him and blushed at his amused smile.

"If you move it any farther away, I'll be in the next county." He patted the ground next to him. "Come, sit beside me."

"I'm too antsy to sit."

"Suit yourself. I'm going to turn in soon. Did you want to get changed? I'll turn my back."

She hesitated for a moment. "I'll change under the covers."

"Nonsense. Here I'll hold up the blanket and you can get changed. I won't look."

She grabbed her gown and a blanket and waited for Tramp to stand. She handed him the blanket. "No peeking."

"Yes, ma'am." He held up the blanket and turned his head.

She hurried as fast as she could, while constantly checking to be sure he didn't look over the blanket. "You must think me silly. I mean we are going to be married tomorrow, but I don't know…the whole thing makes me nervous." She finished changing and hurried to slip under the covers.

Tramp laid the blanket back on his bedroll. "It's only natural to be nervous. It's a big step and shouldn't be taken lightly." He began to take off his boots.

"We aren't taking it lightly, are we? I mean, you do like me, don't you?" She held her breath while waiting for his answer.

"Of course, I like you. Ilene, this has nothing to do with the house or saving your reputation. Those things matter, but not enough to tie myself to one person."

He took off his shirt, and her jaw dropped. She'd never seen muscles like his. He was well chiseled with a sprinkling of dark hair on his chest. She shouldn't look, but she couldn't turn away.

"But you're tying yourself to me."

"Because I care for you. You make my days better." He climbed into his bedroll, which he moved closer to her and the fire. "Good night."

"Good night." He snored lightly and she smiled. I make his days better. Maybe she was supposed to say something back. Dang it all, she was too awkward to be his wife. She'd just embarrass him wherever they went. Her heart squeezed. She wanted to spend the rest of her life with him. She tossed and turned for what seemed like hours before she finally slept.

The heavenly smell of coffee woke her, and she sat up, stretching her arms above her head. Tramp sat with his back against a nearby boulder, watching her. His hair was mussed from sleep and he looked very appealing. "Good morning."

His smile was wide and it went straight to her heart. "Good morning."

"How long have you been up?"

Tramp rose and poured her a cup of coffee. Leaning down, he handed it to her. Then he refilled his own cup and sat back down. "I was up with the sun. I tended Gold Dust. I was surprised she let me near her. She ate some. I'm trying small but frequent feedings. Then I made coffee, and I've been watching you sleep. Did you know you snore?"

"Snore? I think you're imagining it. You're the one who snores."

He laughed. "I probably do." His laughter faded to a tender smile. "You're as pretty as a picture when you sleep."

Her face heated. "You've seen me sleeping plenty of times. You don't have to give me compliments. I don't expect them."

"But you should, expect them I mean. You're probably just not used to them but you deserve them. You can ask anyone. I'm not one to give out compliments. You're very pretty. I like the way your eyes sparkle when you're mad. Your hair is glorious too."

"Glorious? Are you serious?" She didn't wait for an answer. "I'm going to go to the pond and wash my face. I'll be right back." She got up and wrapped the blanket around her then hurried off. Kneeling on the bank, she peered into the water and studied her reflection. She wasn't bad looking. But glorious? He was just trying to put her in a good mood. It was their wedding day, after all. She washed her face and returned to camp.

Tramp stood as she walked back into camp. He held a package in his hands. "Shannon sent this for you."

Taking the offered package she quickly untied it. Inside was the most beautiful lilac dress she'd ever seen. It was much too good for the likes of her to wear. Holding it up against herself, she looked down at it in awe. It looked like a high society ball gown. "Oh my."

"Shannon made it for you."

"It's the nicest dress I've ever seen." She turned it this way and that examining the fine stitching. Tears filled her eyes. "I hope I do it justice by wearing it."

"You'll be the most beautiful bride ever."

Once again, she had him hold up the blanket as she dressed.

This time, she didn't peek at him while he put on clean shirt. Not that she wasn't tempted. "They should be here soon, don't you think?" She tidied the campsite, trying to hide her nervousness by keeping busy.

"That they should. Ilene, stop fussing." He stood in front of her and took both her hands in his. "I will be a good husband to you. You don't have to worry, and I will never make you scream in pain. I want us to have a good life together. Does that help? I want this to be a wonderful day that we will remember forever."

"I guess I am a bundle of nerves. Having you here with me helps. I'll be a good wife to you, Tramp. I care for you too."

Tramp pulled her into his arms and was just about to kiss her when they heard the wagons coming their way. They stood side-by-side, holding hands as they watched all the wagons approach.

"Tramp, I thought it would just be the preacher with

Cinders and Shannon. I thought Cookie might come but who are all these people?"

"It looks like the whole town showed up to help us celebrate."

She frowned. "They came to watch. They came to make sure we are properly wed, they came out of curiosity. They didn't come to wish us happy."

"Shane and Cecily are here, and Keegan's brood is here as well. You like them."

"I don't think I can do this, Tramp. There are too many people. I don't do well in crowds." Her own voice sounded odd to her.

Tramp turned her so she was facing him. "It's just about you and me. These other people don't matter. We want to be wed and if need be we'll ride off after the ceremony. Cinders will watch Gold Dust. We can do this, together. Honey, we can do anything as long as we have each other."

Tears formed in her eyes. He was such a good man, a generous man, a loving man. "As long as I have you I can do it."

He smiled at her and she thought she saw love in his eyes. "That's my girl. Now smile, we have company."

Smile, she did. She smiled as they all drove up and got out of their wagons. She smiled when a few of them actually talked to them. She smiled throughout the ceremony, and she smiled when Tramp kissed her. After that, the smiles were easy to give.

It was uplifting to be on the receiving end of smiles too. Edith only smiled at Cookie but Ilene didn't care.

One last wagon headed their way. It was Poor Boy all cleaned up. My he was handsome. She elbowed Tramp who looked up, saw Poor Boy and nodded. "Right on time."

Before she even had a chance to ask Tramp what he meant Poor Boy drove the horses to them and as soon as he set the break and tied the lines, he hopped down. "The food is here. Eats sends his best to you, Tramp, and you too, Miss Ilene."

Tramp shook the boy's hand and patted him on the back. "Thanks, Poor Boy. I knew I could count on you."

Poor boy blushed and gazed at the ground. "Eats did most of the work." He shuffled his feet back. "I will get the food unloaded." He started to run but turned back. He took a small bag out of his pocket and handed it to Ilene. "Ava gave me this to give to you. She said to say she was sorry."

Ilene gasped. "My money. Thank you, Poor Boy."

Poor Boy gave her a quick nod and rushed off again.

Tramp reached out and gave her hand a squeeze. "You didn't have to marry me after all. You have your money back." He let go of her hand and stared at her.

"You aren't trying to be rid of me so quickly are you?" She tilted her head as she watched him.

He gave her a kiss on the cheek. "Never."

Ilene peered up at Tramp. "You knew that all these people were coming didn't you?"

Tramp winked at her. "I just figured as much. Well, Mrs. Hart, shall we?" He grabbed her hand and pulled her into the midst of the crowd.

A moment of panic jolted through her. None of these people liked her. Almost all had talked about her at one point or another. But she was polite and greeted each and every guest. Glancing up, she was surprised to see Ava standing alone by a tree. She had a tragic look on her face, and Ilene wondered about her sanity. Ilene touched Tramp's arm and motioned with a nod of her head where Ava was. "I thought they were gone."

His brow furrowed. "I thought so too. Well as long as she doesn't cause any trouble, I guess she can watch. I don't want to make a scene by asking her to leave. At least you have your money back. Let's just forget about her."

"Perhaps she needed to know you were really married so she could move on."

"That makes sense. Let's go eat. I'm starved. Then I'm going to check on Gold Dust again. I'm not sure she's appreciating the crowd."

"I know how she feels," she murmured.

"What?"

Ilene smiled. "Nothing. Let's enjoy our day." She held her head up high as Tramp escorted her to the food table. Imagine a wedding in the middle of nowhere. She'd get through being in a crowd with Tramp by her side. He made her feel brave.

TRAMP'S HEART WAS FULL. He was proud to have Ilene as his wife. Best of all, her smile was real. He'd seen plenty of fake smiles to know the difference and it gave him a jolt inside. He did observe her appearing pensive a time or two. Could she be thinking about the wedding night?

He leaned over and kissed her cheek. "I need to talk to Cinders for a minute. I'll be right back." As he made his way to Cinders, Tramp shook a lot of hands. The townspeople seemed sincere, and he was glad for Ilene's sake.

Cinders slapped him on the back. "So, how does it feel to be a married man?"

"That's why I'm here. How did you make Shannon comfortable enough?"

Cinders' brow furrowed. "Comfortable?" A look of understanding crossed his face. "Are we talking about the wedding night?"

Tramp put his weight on one leg then the other. "Yes.

She's scared out of her mind. I'm not sure if I'd know the right words to reassure her. I guess there was a lot of screaming in the tenements she grew up in."

"I'll have Shannon talk to her. Maybe once she knows how good it is she won't be frightened."

"I'd appreciate it." Tramp shook Cinders' hand and wove his way back through the crowd to Ilene. She was surrounded by Shannon, Cecily and Addy and they were talking in hushed tones. From the deep blush on Ilene's face, he knew what they were talking about. He only hoped it helped. Guess he hadn't needed to ask Cinders after all.

He walked to the circle of women and nodded. "Mind if I whisk my beautiful wife away?" He didn't wait for an answer, but grasped Ilene's hand, and someone started playing the fiddle. He immediately took her into his arms and danced with her. It felt so right to have her in his embrace. Upon pulling her closer, he could feel the fast tattoo of her heart. It matched his.

Soon enough, the party wound down. He was finally alone with his bride, and he didn't have a clue what to do next. "We might as well check on Gold Dust." He waited for her nod, and they strolled hand in hand toward the horse.

This time Gold Dust easily allowed Tramp to pick up her foot and examine it. "She's healing."

"She does look better." Ilene kept smoothing out her dress. She was nervous all right.

"Would you like to talk for a while?" At her nod, Tramp led her to a fallen tree, and they both sat on it.

Tramp cleared his throat. "You really don't know much about me. I grew up in a whore house. My mother was a whore. From the time I could first remember I swept the floors and kept the tables gleaming." He paused and ran his hand down his face. "I left when I heard them scheming to sell me to a man for the night. I hightailed it out of there. I was seven. I traveled around some; mostly I hid in wagons and hitched a ride. The last wagon was Cinders' father's. He knew I was there the whole time. It was just him and Cinders. They never talked about what happened to Mrs. Cinders. They just said she was gone." Aware of her rapt attention he continued. "Mr. Cinders took me in and Cinders and I were raised together. It was a fine time. I learned how to ride, rope and drive cattle. I learned a lot about horses. They never lie. All the women I knew were liars and cheats, just like my own mother."

He glanced at the horizon swallowing hard. "Then came Charlotte. She lived on the ranch next to ours. I was so smitten with her that I'd do just about anything she asked. I was bitter when she married Cinders instead of me. There was a darkness to me that I didn't even know existed. The one woman I knew who I believed didn't lie turned out to be the biggest liar and cheat."

"Oh, Tramp, I'm so sorry."

"There's more, and I hope you won't think you made a mistake marrying me. Charlotte asked me to drive her to the banker's house one Saturday. I obliged, but when she asked me to wait in the wagon, I knew. I knew she was cheating on Cinders. All the while when I drove her back and forth, she kept telling me it was me she really loved. I was so stupid and blind I believed her."

Touching his knee she gave it a gently squeeze. "It sounds like she had a lot of people fooled."

"I betrayed my best friend, and when Shannon came along, I assumed her to be like all the other women I knew. I called her a whore and treated her badly. I'll forever be ashamed by my actions."

"I'm sorry all that happened, Tramp. You have to admit you've changed. You made amends with both Cinders and

Shannon. I know you were a bit suspicious of me, but you never treated me horribly."

"I could have been nicer."

"I agree, but we muddled through, and here we are, married. Are you sorry we were pushed into this marriage?"

He cupped her cheek in his palm. "No, I'm not sorry. You've opened my eyes and my heart. I love you with all my heart."

A tear rolled down her face onto his hand. "I love you too. I think I have for a long time. If it hadn't annoyed me so much I would have thought your matchmaking ploys to be funny."

His face heated. "That was a disaster. I can be hard headed at times."

She laughed. "No. Really? You?"

Tramp stood. "I'm going to grab some wood for tonight. It's almost time for the sun to set." Bending down he gave her a heart-searing kiss. Then he went into the woods, hoping to give her time alone to prepare for the night to come.

HER HANDS SHOOK as she tried to take in the whole day. It certainly had turned out much different from what she'd thought. People seemed to accept her, but the best part besides Tramp was having friends. Shannon, Addy, and Cecily all came to make sure she wasn't frightened about her wedding night. They each agreed it was one of the best parts of marriage. When she asked about the screams and pleading she was used to, they told her some men don't make sure a woman is ready. They were all sure Tramp would take his time.

Standing, she stretched her back. She trusted him, and that was all she could do, trust in him. She hoped she didn't have reason to cry. Even with the reassurances she was nervous. If she could keep the sun high in the sky she would. But alas, it sunk lower and lower. Dusk was upon her. There was leftover food but she didn't feel like eating. Her stomach was in knots.

She walked over to Gold Dust and patted her neck. "You trust him, don't you? He's a good man. He's kind to me and he seems to know my fears before I do. I love him with my whole heart. I really don't know how it happened. It just snuck up on me." She gave the horse one final pat. "You're right, it'll be fine."

"Talking to the horse again?" The humor in Tramp's eyes calmed her and she laughed.

"I was asking if she liked you."

"Well?" Tramp walked toward her until they stood toe to toe.

"She said yes." She sounded breathless.

"Smart horse." Tramp pulled her closer until they were touching. "Come, let's make a fire and go to bed."

By the huskiness of his voice she didn't think sleeping was what he had planned. Reluctantly she moved out of the circle of his arms and walked to the fire pit. Tramp joined her and had a fire going in no time. The firelight playing off his hair made him look even more handsome.

She placed both bedrolls side by side. "Will you hold up the blanket so I can change?"

"No, honey, I want to see all of you." His eyes were full of desire.

"Will I get to see you too?"

"I wouldn't have it any other way." He knelt on the bedroll and waited for her to do the same.

He wrapped his arms around her and he smelled of the outdoors and everything good. His shoulders seemed bigger than ever. He loosened his hold and stared into her eyes. Her heart raced as they stared at each other. He began to unbutton his shirt and she was a goner.

SHE WOKE the next morning feeling loved and so safe in Tramps arms. Her friends had been right, it had been a very moving experience. He stirred, opened his eyes and smiled.

"Well hello, Mrs. Hart. How do you feel? Are you sore?"

Her face heated but she held his gaze. "I feel so loved. My heart is so full, and I've never been happier. I love you!"

He rolled them until she was flat on her back. "We don't have to get up just yet." His smile made her stomach flip.

EPILOGUE

 *ne Month Later*

"Do I look all right?" Ilene asked Tramp as she smoothed out her skirt.

"You're fine. You'll just be sewing."

"No, it's the first time I'm hosting the bee."

"They were here before." Tramp poured himself a cup of coffee.

"That wasn't hosting, it was just here because I couldn't leave the house. But now it's really my house I want to make a good impression."

Tramp put his cup down and rounded the table until he reached her. "I don't know if I'm the one you should ask."

She frowned. "What does that mean?"

"I can't be objective about you. You are my sunshine during the day and my stars at night. You've brightened my life, and somehow you've made me feel whole. You could be covered in mud and I'd still think you beautiful. I love everything you've done to the house right down to those prissy doilies you made."

"Prissy?" She cocked her head as she stared at her handsome husband.

"Yes, but I love them because you made them. Don't worry about the other women. You're all friends anyway." He grimaced. "Well, maybe not Edith. Last I heard she was trying to get Poor Boy to go to school."

"Oh no. Poor Boy is old enough to decide for himself. Besides He's filled out and doesn't have that haunted look in his eyes anymore. A change for the better. He'll make something of his life."

"Always the optimist except for when it comes to yourself. You are the kindest, smartest, and loveliest woman I know and don't you forget it. Don't forget, tomorrow we find that black stallion."

Ilene wrapped her arms around his waist. "I was thinking about that stallion. He's outfoxed us so many times and I think we should let him stay free. I did pick up tracks of another herd. I'd sure love to try my luck at finding them."

He kissed the top of her head. "You've turned my world upside down, and I've loved every minute of it. A different herd it is. I really thought it'd be a hardship to work the horses with you but you've got what it takes. You make me proud to be your husband. I hear a wagon." He gave her a lingering kiss and then lit out.

Ilene touched her tingling lips with her fingers. That man sure could kiss her senseless. Looking around she felt grateful for all she had. Especially for a man who liked doilies just because she made them. She'd found her happily ever after.

THE END

I'm so pleased you chose to read Tramp's Bride, and it's my sincere hope that you enjoyed the story. I would appreciate if you'd consider posting a review. This can help an author tremendously in obtaining a readership. My many thanks. ~ Kathleen

ABOUT THE AUTHOR

Sexy Cowboys and the Women Who Love Them...
Finalist in the 2012 and 2015 RONE Awards.
Top Pick, Five Star Series from the Romance Review.
Kathleen Ball writes contemporary and historical western
romance with great emotion and
memorable characters. Her books are award winners and
have appeared on best sellers lists including: Amazon's Best
Seller's List, All Romance Ebooks, Bookstrand, Desert
Breeze Publishing and Secret Cravings Publishing Best
Sellers list. She is the recipient of eight Editor's Choice
Awards, and The Readers' Choice Award for Ryelee's
Cowboy.
Winner of the Lear diamond award Best Historical Novel-
Cinders' Bride
There's something about a cowboy

facebook.com/kathleenballwesternromance

twitter.com/kballauthor

instagram.com/author_kathleenball

So Many Roads to Choose

The Settlers

Greg

Juan

Scarlett

Mail Order Brides of Spring Water

Tattered Hearts

Shattered Trust

Glory's Groom

Battered Soul

The Greatest Gift

Love So Deep

Luke's Fate

Whispered Love

Love Before Midnight

I'm Forever Yours

Finn's Fortune

Glory's Groom

Made in the USA
Columbia, SC
30 May 2023